THE YELLOW SHADOW

This copy, then, is for
Sova & John Michael
in thanks for all the
conversations & — in the
Light of all journeys - far
West to east to west.

Ex Oriente Lux —
across the international
dateline!

VIOLET MARY FIRTH, DION FORTUNE AND V. M. STEELE

MANY people know the name Dion Fortune, which was the pseudonym used by Violet Mary Firth to pen her occult novels; *The Demon Lover, The Winged Bull, The Goat-Foot God, The Sea Priestess,* and *Moon Magic.*

What is less well known is that Violet Mary Firth had another persona; V. M. Steele, the writer of romantic thrillers. As V. M. Steele she completed four novels; *The Scarred Wrists, Hunters of Humans, Beloved of Ishmael* and *The Yellow Shadow.* Though she is well known for her occult novels, she is almost completely unknown for her thrillers.

The Yellow Shadow was published in 1942, and is, to modern political correctness, quite shocking. The opening paragraph starts with a description of the heroine's landlady as taking exception to the 'yellow Chinaman' who had been retained by the girl's dying father to teach her Chinese. The prejudices of the British, especially in relation to their colonial ambitions are laid bare as the reader follows the exploits of young Stella Morris.

Violet Firth's parents came from a family that made its fortune in Sheffield, manufacturing steel for armaments, so it is interesting to note how the pseudonym V. M. Steele combines the names Violet and Mary with Steele (as a nod to the source of the family's fortune). The Firth motto was *'Deo, non fortuna'* ('God, not luck'), which was later used by Violet as her magical name, Dion Fortune.

The Yellow Shadow

by

V. M. Steele

Author of
The Scarred Wrists,
Beloved of Ishmael
and Hunters of Humans

First published 1942 by Morrison and Gibb Ltd., printers, Tanfield, Edinburgh, and published by Quality Press Ltd., 22 Essex Street, Strand, London, WC2.

V. M. Steele was one of the pseudonyms used by V M Firth, more commonly known as Dion Fortune.

Library and Archives Canada Cataloguing in Publication

Steele, V. M., author
   The yellow shadow / by V. M. Steele

ISBN 978-1-896238-19-7 (softcover)

   1. Title

PR6011.172Y45 2017   **823'.912**   **C2017-901544-3**

TWIN EAGLES PUBLISHING

Box 2031
Sechelt BC
V0N 3A0

pblakey@telus.net

twineaglespublishing.com

2017

CHAPTER I

MRS. CRAGGS, being a Bloomsbury lady, was accustomed to tolerate in a good deal of eccentricity on the part of her lodgers, but when Miss Morris engaged a yellow Chinaman to come twice a week to teach her Chinese, she put her foot down. It is true that Mr. Fook, if appearances were anything to go by, was a exceedingly ancient and intensely respectable, but Mrs. Craggs was convinced that in his case appearances were nothing to go by, him being yellow and therefore a peril to any English girl he looked at twice out of his narrow eyes. Mr. Fook, having raised a Eurasian family in the Commercial Road, knew all there was to know about race prejudice, and was quite alive to her attitude. He was equally quite indifferent. Miss Morris was also quite indifferent, being used to coping with landladies. Likewise Mr. Morris, who had been a desk-mate of Mr. Fook's for years in the British Museum reading-room and knew that he was as likely to behave with impropriety as the statue from Easter Island that decorates its front steps. So Mrs. Craggs had to retire to her underground den breathing threats and beer-fumes and dark prophecies, no one paying any attention to her.

Of course Mrs. Craggs was perfectly right it was a very odd arrangement—and no one but a bat-eyed scholar would have dreamt of it. Mr. Morris, knowing that his days were numbered by an inoperable cancer, and that after his death his daughter would go out to her aunt in southern China, was, with what he fondly believed to be foresight, having her taught Chinese, not realising that a young English girl living in a wealthy household in a Concession, has about as much use for the Chinese language there as here. Nor did Mr. Fook enlighten him, the five shillings he got for a lesson being very welcome to the poverty-stricken copyist of Oriental languages.

During the long days and longer nights while Stella nursed her father after he took to his bed, she toiled at her Chinese grammar and phrase-book. Old Fook, who had taught many young men going out to take up positions in commercial houses and the government service, was enraptured at her progress, for she, poor child, had no distractions to take her mind off her studies. He, in fact, was her only distraction, and the bi-weekly visits of the kind old Chinaman the only relief she had from the lonely waiting for the inevitable end that was so slow in coming. He was the only person she had to talk to during the last long weeks when her father lay in the merciful twilight of morphia, and between the old yellow man and the young white girl there sprang up a deep sympathy and warm affection, and it was his calm Confucian philosophy that steadied her during the last bad hours.

She had just taken a final farewell of him, which they had both felt keenly. The little old man had called for her, and carried her suit-case to the station, thus saving her a taxi (Mrs. Craggs being firmly convinced that at last they were eloping), and had put her on the dingy train for the Docks— the train that amid the popping of fog-signals, was crawling laboriously down the fog-bound riverside line. An ominous absence of hooting from the river told that all water traffic was at a standstill. A more ex-perienced traveller than Stella would have rung up the shipping company before setting out on such a fog-bound pilgrimage.

Her heavy luggage had gone on by Carter Paterson, and she had nothing but her suit-case to cope with—luckily for her, for there was no one but a ticket-collector at the station where she finally got out, and the ticket-collector seemed very surprised to see her, and very doubtful what to do with her when she en-quired her way to the shipping company's pier.

"Wait a minute, miss," he said, "I'll see if there's anybody else for the boat."

There did not appear to be, and he was scratching his head dubiously, when out of the mists there loomed up the figure of a man in an ulster, collar turned up to his ears, Homburg hat pulled down to his eyes, at his heels a meek Chinese man servant, who enquired in the voice of one accustomed to exercise authority why there was no one from the ship to meet the train and take off luggage?

The ticket-collector explained that the sailing had been postponed on account of the fog. The newcomer demanded that the ship should be telephoned forthwith and bidden to send stewards to cope with luggage. The ticket-collector replied that she was still lying out in the river and could not be telephoned. The guard came up and demanded indignantly that the ticket-collector should lend a hand with the luggage, and followed by the Chinese valet, they disappeared into the gloom leaving Stella and the stranger alone together under the dim lamp of the gateway. The stranger turned and walked slowly off down the platform into the shadows; evidently he had no taste for making the acquaintance of damsels travelling unescorted. She was sorry for this, for she had liked his voice, and had hoped she might make a pleasant travelling acquaintance, It was a cultured voice, and its Oxford accent did not sound affected. Its precise utterance was that which is habitual to a scholar, She had heard many such voices among the men who came to visit her father. It was, perhaps a trifle high-pitched, but it had the restraint of a man who is a gentleman as well as a scholar, and she could not imagine it ever being raised in anger. The stranger, she thought, was an Oxford don of some standing; probably a man who, in addition to his academic qualifications, was also of good family, for he had that air of serene poise and authority that breeding, and nothing but breeding, gives.

Stella waited patiently under the lamp for the reappearance of the ticket-collector. The stranger had disappeared. Presently there appeared out of the gloom some exceedingly unsavoury long-shore loungers, who proceeded to pile a quantity of expensive-looking luggage onto a hand-truck under the supervision of the Chinese man-servant. The ticket-collector appeared from out of the shadows and stuck Stella's suit-case on top of the pile. The Chinese valet protested.

"Garn," said the ticket-collector, "your governor'll oblige a lady."

The Chinese valet appeared to think otherwise. Then out of the gloom appeared his master, suddenly, as if he had been all the time near at hand. He startled Stella, he appeared so suddenly.

The ticket-collector appealed to him.

"Will you take the young lady with you, sir? She's for the boat, and she didn't ought to go alone."

"Certainly," said the stranger, bowing and raising his hat to Stella. Evidently the valet had been misinformed.

Followed by the luggage on its clanking truck shoved by the objurgating loafers, they made their way up a long, sloping asphalt path lit at rare intervals by gas-lamps. Then they crossed an apparently endless foot-bridge over railway sidings, and down another long asphalt slope. Finally they arrived at the gates of a pier. Not a soul was in sight, nor any sign of light or life; but the loafers all set themselves to hallooing, and presently footsteps rang hollow on the planking, and a jersey-clad individual, with the shipping company's initials decorating his chest, came and peered at them through the bars of the gate. Stella's new acquaintance proffered papers and demanded admittance; but the guardian of the gate shook his head. The ship was not yet alongside, and there was nothing to be done. After some argument he accepted responsibility for the luggage, unlocked the gate, and allowed it to be put inside a shed; but he would accept no responsibility for the human portion of the ship's prospective freight, and shut the gate firmly in their faces.

"This is exceedingly tiresome," said Stella's companion, with an academic calm that belied his words. Stella shyly agreed. She had had very little social experience during her nineteen motherless years in Bloomsbury lodgings, and this was not a man with whom it was easy to make friends. He had the gift of silence, which he apparently expected his companion to share without embarrassment. The pier-hand had disappeared into the murk. The longshoremen had taken their tip and departed hastily lest any other job should come their way before the cash had been changed into beer, and the Chinese valet was as taciturn and immobile as his own joss—and about as helpful. The gas-lamp over their heads shed a small cone of light down upon them, and all around was shadowy gloom filled with drifting fog-wreaths.

They turned and made their way back to the station— there was nothing else to be done, the railway company had fenced its property securely, and on every side there were six-foot fences made of old sleepers with nails on top.

But when they arrived back at the station they were no better off, for the station staff had shut up shop and gone home, no more trains apparently being expected at the moment. The place was in darkness and silent as the tomb.

Stella's companion produced a big electric torch from a despatch case, and guided by its beam, they made their way across the footbridge to the up-platform, where the booking office presented a blank face to a fog-bound world. They peered in through the glass panels of the door of the refreshment room, and saw the glimmer of extinguished urns in the darkness, and pale glass domes that probably sheltered sandwiches. Stella's companion turned and addressed his valet in his own language. The valet produced a pocket knife, did something at the keyhole, and the door swung open.

They walked into the clammy gloom. The valet, suddenly transformed into an Admirable Crichton, lit the gas; disappeared behind the refreshment counter into the back premises; reappeared with an armful of kindling; and in less time than it takes to tell, had a blazing fire going in the capacious railway grate, having made use of what was probably the official ration of kindling for the rest of the week; then he placed two straight-backed, leather-seated chairs beside the hearth and disappeared once more into the back premises, where the pop of a gas-ring, speedily followed by the singing of a kettle, showed that refreshments would soon be available.

Stella and her companion seated themselves and put their feet on the fender. She noted that his rather large feet were cased in expensive looking shoes and that his socks were of silk. More of him she could not note, for he had not seen fit to remove his

9

hat in the fog-filled waiting-room, and the light being directly over his head, she could see no more than that he was clean-shaven, Stella herself, in her beret, had the hard glare full in her eyes. She tried to shield them with her hand, for the fierce white light hurt them.

"A most unpleasant glare," said her companion, noticing her action, and rose and pulled down the chain that extinguished the old-fashioned lamp—the fire, liberally fed with the Company's coal, giving ample light. Then, for the first time, it seemed to occur to him that he owed his companion some thing more than his silent presence, and he offered her a cigarette. The valet returned with a pot of tea. It was, she noted as he poured it out, extremely weak. His employer apologised.

"I am afraid your tastes have not been considered in the making of this tea," he said. Stella explained that she too took her tea weak, but with sugar and milk, which had not been placed on the tray. Sugar was produced, and they settled down to a meal of ham sandwiches, currant buns, and the hot rank liquid that passes with railway companies for tea. Weak as it was, it rasped the tongue.

"To make good tea strong is to insult it," said Stella's companion; "and the less one tastes of bad tea, the better," and he added still more water to his cup. " You are not, I take it, a connoisseur of tea?" he said with a smile, as Stella added more sugar to hers to mask its flavour.

"I am not a connoisseur of anything," said Stella. " My speciality is adaptability."

This middle-aged don was the kind of man she was accustomed to. She could deal with him; whereas she was all at sea with boys of her own age, who disliked her because her wit was too keen, and her outlook on life too serious, and she knew none of the current clichés. Neither did they consider her calm, oval face, with its large dark eyes and madonna hair at all attractive when compared with lipstick and perms.

She had been a distinctly plain child, with her colourless skin, snub nose, and straight dark hair; neither had she been an attractive flapper, being gauche with shyness; but as she matured into womanhood her looks, in the words of one of the landladies, 'grew on you.' The dark hair became darker, and the colourless skin cleared and grew creamy; nevertheless, she ' was never one for the boys,' as the same landlady had remarked. Her father's friends liked her wit and intelligence, and she liked their old-fashioned courtesy that matched her own old-fashioned staidness—the staidness of a child that has known no other children. She liked their talk, too, for she had inherited her father's brains. Had her companion been a presentable young man she would not have known what to say to him, but she could cope with middle-aged dons—they were right along her own line of country.

She knew from experience that nothing was easier than to make friends with middle aged or elderly men by the exercise of little more than common kindness. Stella was not coquettish, and did not realise the way in which her innocent wish to make friends fluttered the middle-aged male heart, long unaccustomed to female blandishments. As innocently as she would have thawed one of her father's fellow scholars, she set to work to make friends with her taciturn companion, who was her fellow prisoner until such time as the railway company saw fit to reopen its premises for the rush-hour traffic in the evening. The only friends she had ever known were just such men as this—absent minded and aloof scholars blinking like owls in the unaccustomed light of feminine society.

Stella knew better than to expect them to meet her halfway—she just paid no attention to their gaucheness but took it for granted there was a human being behind all the dusty learning; and invariably there was, and often an unexpectedly charming human being.

Using her innocent technique, Stella set to work to make friends with her new acquaintance She told him of her father and his work trying to discover along what line the strangers learning lay But he merely displayed polite interest in John Morris's fame, his name being apparently unknown to him.

Stella challenged him with being an Oxford man, and this he admitted. She asked him if he were connected with the University, but this he denied.

"That is odd," said Stella, " I could have sworn you were an Oxford don."

"It is curious that you should say that," said her companion, "for it is what I would have been if I had had my choice."

"What did you take your degree in?" asked Stella, claiming a scholar's privilege, even if one generation removed.

"International law. Then I did post-graduate work in economics, but I could not proceed to my doctorate as my father died unexpectedly and I had to go home and take charge of the family business. I am a banker," he added.

"In China?" asked Stella.

"In China, and wherever business is done with China—the Straits Settlements, San Francisco, Vancouver, Australia."

Stella asked no more questions. She had claimed a scholar's privilege in questioning him about his line of work, but she could not question him about his business. He, however, the ice being broken, turned the tables on her, and she found herself telling him all her family history. She told him of her odd, motherless upbringing among the scholars.

"That was how I knew you were a scholar of some sort," she said.

"But you were wrong," said her companion, "I am no more a scholar than any other man who comes down with his degree. I am a business man, plain and simple."

"Oh no, you're not. You're something more than that," said Stella.

"Well, perhaps I may claim to some interest in politics. It is hardly possible to be a banker in my part of the world and not be interested in politics."

"And what is your line in politics?"

"I have no line, save to try and prevent China from collapsing altogether into anarchy." "And do you think you will be able to manage it?"

"God knows. One can only try. One cannot, in common decency, do less than one's best."

Then he gathered the conversation back into his own hands

again, and asked her what was taking her to China, and she told him of her father's long illness, and Mr. Fook and her Chinese studies in preparation for the time when she would go to live with her mother's relations in a treaty port.

"Then in that case," said her companion, " I am afraid that Mr. Fook, kind as he was, swindled you, for you will never have any occasion to make use of your Chinese. The servants will all speak pidgin, and you will never meet a native socially."

"But how odd," said Stella, "to live in a country, and yet never come in touch with it."

"That is how English people live in China, for the most part," he replied. "You will never go outside the Concession, except, perhaps, for a picnic, and the Chinese never come in except to do business, But let me test your Chinese," he continued, and addressing her formally in that language, he asked her how long she expected to reside in China. The unfamiliar voice made it a little difficult for her to catch the soft-sounding words, but she was able to follow his meaning well enough, and replied in due form.

"You speak correctly and with a good accent," he answered in English; "but you address me as if I were your grandfather, You have not been taught the correct modes of address."

Stella felt rather crestfallen, for Mr. Fook had taken great pains with her manners. She knew all the proper forms, but had thought that this scholarly man so much older than herself should be addressed as a reverent senior.

"Nor do I think you are right in thinking you are to live permanently with your aunt," he added; "for English girls are as scarce and precious in China as Chinese women in Limehouse. You will be married before you know where you are."

"I don't think so," said Stella. " I do not get on well with boys. They don't like me, and I don't like them. I get on better with older men, and they are usually appropriated by the time they are old enough to appreciate me. You see, I am not pretty, and I'm under no delusions on the subject"

Her companion did not answer for a moment. Then, when he spoke, there was a curious change in his voice. "Europeans may not admire you, Miss Morris, but you Will find that the Chinese Will consider you beautiful—very beautiful," he added.

"That will be a new experience," said Stella. "But as you say I won't be meeting any Chinese, I don't suppose it will make much difference."

Then her companion shifted the talk from personalities to politics, and they talked of shirts of all shades, and the folly of doctrinaires who take no account of human nature. Stella, who had learnt to read in the columns of The Times, could more than hold her own here, and soon had her companion arguing in earnest as if with a man of his own standing; then, her quick wit flashing out, she had him laughing—and the Chinese valet popped a startled face out of the kitchen at the sound.

Time went quickly under such circumstances, and they were taken by surprise when they heard heavy footsteps and agitated voices on the platform as the station staff, returning to open up for the evening traffic, jumped to the conclusion that the refreshment room had been burgled.

They learnt that, unnoticed by them, the fog had cleared, and that although the ship was not yet alongside the pier, it was possible to get out to her in a row-boat.

So they set off again on their weary Via Dolorosa, only to learn that row-boats did not ply from the pier. Following the pier-hand's instructions, they made their way by a maze of mean riverside streets till they came to the dock-gates; were admitted on showing their papers and explaining their plight, and set out to follow a line of rails, walking on the sleepers as best they might, Stella stumbling on her high heels at every third step.

"I think you had better take my arm, unless you object," said her companion. Stella did so thankfully, wondering why in the world she should be expected to object, and for the rest of their journey they went arm-in-arm like old friends.

And yet it was not like old friends. Stella had often walked arm-in-arm with her father's friends, usually to guide their doddering footsteps among the traffic, but it was utterly different from walking arm-in-arm with this man, yet she could not define the difference. She felt extraordinarily conscious of his personality, and in a way she known had never with any other person. She felt, also, a strange lighting-up of her own personality. What he felt, she did not know, for from the time she took his arm till they reached the quay, he never opened his lips.

He gave her his hand to help her down the slippery water- side steps and into the boat; and up the swaying accommodation-ladder onto the ship's deck. There they were met by a quarter-master, who bade them go into the lounge and he would send the purser to them. He disappeared down the half-lit decks, and they stepped into the brilliantly lighted but empty lounge.

Stella turned to her companion. "By the way, you have never told me your name," she said.

"My name is Lee, and I spell it with an I," was the answer.

"With an I ?" said Stella mystified.

"Yes, Li." He bared his head under the bright light, and Stella found herself looking up into the expressionless yellow face of a Chinaman.

"I think I will see about the baggage," said Mr. Li, and turned and went out onto the dark deck, leaving Stella alone to await the purser.

CHAPTER II

The purser, who looked as if he either drank or suffered with his digestion, possibly both—dealt with Stella's papers, eyed her sharply, and handed her over to a stewardess with a non-committal face. The stewardess led her down steep stairs, and down again; then along a narrow alley-way and into a brightly lit, white-painted cabin. It looked pleasant, but felt stuffy. Stella expressed pleasure at its white cleanness.

"But it is rather airless," she said. "Where is the window?"

"There's no window," said the stewardess grimly. "Not even a port-hole. It's an inside cabin."

"Oh dear," said Stella, "how do I get fresh air?"

The stewardess did not answer for a moment, then she said:

"If you don't like your cabin, miss, you had better see the purser about changing it."

Back they went along the alley-way, and up the steep stairs, and up again. The purser was in his office with the shutter open. Stella had a feeling that he was waiting for her. She saw a suppressed smile curling the corners of the stewardess's lips. Stella timidly asked if it were possible to exchange her cabin for another.

"Certainly," said the purser, and placed a plan of the ship before her. "This berth is vacant, and this, and this," touching the little squares on the plan with his pencil. "This one will be fifteen pounds in addition to the fare you have paid; this one is twenty, and this twenty-five."

"Oh dear," exclaimed Stella, "I am afraid I can't manage it. Isn't there a cooler cabin at the same price?"

"No," said the purser. "I am afraid there isn't. That cabin is

16

the cheapest on the ship on account of its drawbacks. What will you do? Will you pay the extra and have one of these others?"

"I am afraid I can't," said Stella miserably, "I must just put up with it."

"Very good," said the purser, and slammed down his shutter.

Stella looked at the stewardess, and the stewardess looked at Stella. Neither said anything till they were out of earshot of the office.

"You had better pay, miss, and change over," said the stewardess. "He won't let you have another berth at the same price, not if the whole ship was empty. People do this so often. They know that cabin."

"But I can't manage it," said Stella. "I can't really. I shall have to put up with it."

The stewardess showed Stella how to put the door on the hook so as to get what air there was, and left her.

In a few moments, however, there was a knock at the door, and Stella opened to the steward, bearing a heavily laden tray.

"I thought you would like to have your dinner in here miss. There's no one else on board yet except a Chinese gentleman, and he's having his meal in his suite."

Stella was disappointed. She felt she could have made a real friend of her new acquaintance, even if he were a Chinaman. However, there was nothing else for it, and she settled down very comfortably to the excellent cold meal the steward had brought her. But he evidently did not consider even that piled-up tray to be adequate, and in a few minutes he was along again with a pot of tea.

"I thought you might like this miss," he said, "seeing as you've only 'ad a cold supper."

Stella's spirits, depressed by the ignominy of the cabin incident, rose. The food was too lavish for words, judged by the standard of Bloomsbury lodging-house catering, and both steward and stewardess were evidently disposed to take her under their respective wings. Even the cabin, now that she had taken off her coat and got used to its atmosphere, did not feel unduly hot. She went to bed and slept quite happily.

She was awakened by an infernal din that seemed to come from her very pillow. Reverberating through the metal bulk-head beside her head, heavy boots rang on iron steps as the engine-room staff clattered down the ladders to go on duty. She turned on the light and looked at her watch. It was six o'clock. Evidently she was going to be awakened at six o'clock every morning. But that would be no undue hardship, she could put up with that.

There came a knock at the door, and without waiting for permission, in walked the steward, quite unembarrassed—which was more than could be said for Stella—in his hand a large cup of tea.

"I reckoned the engine-room watch would wake you up when they went on duty, miss," he said. Stella drank her tea gratefully; and then, as the iron stairs beside her head seemed to be taking all the traffic of the district, she got up and dressed, further sleep being impossible.

She went on deck and watched the river unfold in the morning mist. It was a fascinating sight. Fortified by the cup of tea and the large ship's biscuit that accompanied it, she could have watched it, entranced, for hours, oblivious of breakfast. But another steward was at her elbow—the stewards seemed to be making a kind of pet of her, which was very sweet of them, for they must have known from what she had had to admit to the purser that she would not be a lavish tipper.

"I reckoned you'd be up early, miss," said the steward, grinning, "so I've got your breakfast."

She followed him to the dining-saloon where enough food for a school-treat awaited her.   She   hurried through her breakfast, for she felt the ship being got under way, and was up on deck in time to see her berthed at the pier, and the gangways run out, and the shore telephone put in, and the derricks get busy with the heavy baggage—all very thrilling to the untravelled Stella.

She wondered, as she walked the decks in the freshness of the morning, when she would see her Chinese friend again. She had liked him enormously, in spite of the fact that he was a Chinese. Having known and liked Mr. Fook, she did not regard all Chinamen as the murderous villains represented by the movies.

She soon forgot about her new friend, however, in watching the train come onto the quay and the passengers stream aboard, their luggage following them at express speed. Then there was the fascinating progress down the river, with so much to see. In fact, it was not until the bugle summoned her to lunch that she gave him another thought, and then only because she saw him away across the saloon, at the captain's table.

She herself was humbly seated at the table of the chief engineer, a taciturn and bearded Scot, who gulped his way half through the menu and departed, never having opened his mouth except to put something in it. One or two of her neighbours were friendly and pleasant in a mild and tentative way, but Stella's eyes were across the saloon where she could see a calm yellow face, impassive among the white ones, as she wondered how her travelling friendship with the Chinese banker was going to develop. She had always heard that board-ship friendships developed rapidly and never survived the end of the voyage. She wondered whether hers would be an exception to the rule, and whether she would see any thing of Mr. Li after she had landed. She would be very disappointed if she were never to see anything of the native life of the country, but were destined to live entirely among the Europeans in the Concession for she was keenly interested in China and things Chinese, and had read everything she could lay her hands on about them. She wanted to cultivate her acquaintance with Mr. Li so as to have a point of contact with Chinese life.

He had disappeared when she came out from the saloon, and did not show up at tea, nor on deck, where every one was watching the coastwise lights of the Channel. She hoped she would have a word with him at dinner, and preened herself in her simple evening dress, and went early into the lounge, but he passed her unobserving, and again he had finished his meal and left the saloon ahead of her.

But when she got out into the lounge, there he was, held in conversation by the captain. Naturally she could not join in such a conversation as that, but she nodded to him as she passed towards the stairs. He gazed at her blankly with complete non-recognition.

Stella felt as if she had had a slap in the face, and with cheeks burning, scuttled along the alley-way and took refuge in her cabin. So that was what she got for being a fool and over-looking racial distinctions Stella was very cross with herself. She snatched up a wrap and hurried on deck to cool off in the dark and the breeze.

She walked the deck for a while, and then, sleepy from the sea air and her early awakening, she went below, and so to bed.

But not to sleep. She had hardly put her head on the pillow when the ship's bell rang the hour, and immediately there was a deafening clatter beside her head as the watch changed, and a couple of dozen booted men raced up the iron stairs that were only separated from her head by a sheet of resonant steel. And every four hours through the night, with individual clatterings between whiles as the senior engineers went their rounds, the din recurred. At six the steward brought her tea.

"Get any sleep, miss ? " he asked.

"Not much," said the heavy-eyed Stella, clutching the tea-tray thankfully. Was it going to be like this throughout the six weeks of voyage, she asked herself ? No wonder people liked to change that cabin.

All morning she slept in her deck-chair.

"I've got you a quiet corner, miss," said the deck steward in a sympathetic whisper, and she was thankful for it. It had begun to dawn on her that the cabin she occupied was notorious, and that the stewards were very sorry for her. The sympathetic stew-ardess had evidently repeated the conversation with the purser. It was one thing to take that cabin in the hope of getting a transfer to a better one, but quite another to take it and stick it because one just hadn't got the money for anything better. The stewards, she saw, were doing all in their power to minimise her discomfort, and sympathising as openly as they dared.

Mr. Li came out and paced the deck for a while during the afternoon, collar turned up and hat over eyes. He paid no attention to her, and she paid none to him. The deck steward, bringing her a cup of tea, surveyed his retreating back. "

"Fust Chinaman I ever seed take exercise," he commented.

Mr. Li passed and repassed in the gathering dusk, and Stella went to sleep again. She was fed up with him.

Another penitential night dragged by in the cabin that was now like the Black Hole of Calcutta in addition to its soul-destroying din for the ship was being driven to make up for the time lost owing to the fog, the engine-room was warming up, and the hot air rising up the ladder-shaft made the steel bulkhead beside her bunk as hot as a radiator.

Stella got a little sleep towards morning from sheer exhaustion, and rising late, came in for the tail-end of the breakfast. Entering the saloon, she came face to face with Mr. Li, but as he had already given her the cut direct, she returned it, and passed him with a blank, expressionless face as if he did not exist. Then she went on deck and slept in her deck-chair on and off for the rest of the morning.

But sleep snatched like that, between bugling, deck games, and the ship's bell at half-hourly intervals, had no real rest in it, and as Stella went wearily to her cabin after dinner she wondered how in the world she was going to survive for the six long weeks that lay ahead, and whether she would finally get used to the din and sleep through it. But if she got used to the din, would she get used to the heat ? And what was it going to be like as the weather got hotter ? It was like a Turkish bath now—it would be just plain hell then. Reluctantly she entered her cabin, switched on the light, and to her amazement found it completely empty—all her belongings had vanished.

Before she had time to take in the significance of this new catastrophe, a voice said behind her:

"It's all right, miss, you ain't been burgled. We've shifted your cabin." And turned to see her friend the steward behind her with a broad grin on his face.

21

Stella was so relieved that she could hardly keep back the tears.

"Come along with me, miss, and I'll show you your new quarters you've struck it lucky," said the steward.

She followed him down the long alley-way, and up the steep narrow stairs, and along another alley-way into another section of the passage turning at right angles from starboard to port. The steward opened the first door they came to, and ushered her into a large airy cabin that would have held at least three of the one she had vacated. It had a real bed instead of a bunk, and a writing-table and an easy chair, Stella could hardly believe her eyes.

"I told yer you'd struck it lucky," said the grinning steward as she gazed speechlessly at all this luxury.

"I certainly have," said Stella. " I must go and thank the purser at once."

"You better not! You keep out of 'is way. 'E'll kill yer if yer go near 'im. 'E ain't 'aif 'ad 'is tail twisted."

The steward, who evidently did not wish to commit himself to any expression of opinion that could be quoted, faded like the Cheshire Cat, his grin lingering on the air long after he had left.

Stella sat down on the thick silk eiderdown that covered the bed and gazed round at all the glory of ivory paint and rose brocade and satinwood furniture, and tried to guess who had twisted the purser's tail on her behalf. There was a knock on the door; she rose to open it and looked out into the alley-way, but there was no one there. The knock was repeated, and then she saw that the stateroom had a second door, she opened it, and there, with his back to a bath, stood Mr. Li.

"I ask your pardon for intruding on you," said her visitor, who could hardly be said to be intruding, for he was a yard away, in his own bathroom. "But there are things it is necessary I should explain in order to avoid misunderstandings. If you would honour me by coming to my sitting-room, it would give me much pleasure."

Stella, very perplexed, acquiesced. Was it Mr. Li who had

done the tail-twisting? And if so, how had he managed it? And why, after cutting her dead, and being cut dead, had he taken the trouble to interest himself in her welfare?

Stella followed him through the bathroom and into another room, twice the size of her cabin, and furnished as a cross between a sitting-room and an office, The serviceable desk, very different from Stella's Sheraton writing-table, was piled with papers in systematic order; despatch cases stood in a row beside it; files hung from hooks on the walls. Anything less like the opium den to which the orthodox Chinese lures his victim—according to the movies—it would be hard to imagine. Mr. Li bowed her to a large arm-chair and sat down himself at the desk. It was exactly like a visit to a doctor.

It was impossible to associate embarrassment with this man of the world, who combined Oriental calm with European polish, but Stella suspected that, having got her there, he could not decide what to do with her, the opening he had prepared for the interview having evidently gone astray.

He examined his finger-nails. Stella noticed that they were filed to an over-long filbert point after the manner of ultra-smart shop-girls. She felt a sudden sense of repulsion.

The English like directness," said Mr. Li, still examining his nails as if to see that the ship's manicurist had done her work properly. "The Chinese do not ; we think it causes a shock to the system. You are English; I am Chinese; it is very awkward."

Stella, who had no small talk and no social savoir faire, silently agreed with him, but did not help him out.

He looked up suddenly, his eyes two slits, like a cat at noon. "You would like to know why you are here?"

"Yes, please," said Stella.

"My man, who hears everything, had learnt that you had been given that infamous cabin which the Board of Trade ought to condemn—and I saw from your face that it was making you ill. I went to the purser and offered to pay for you to have a better cabin. He refused, saying that was a trick which had been played too often. I assured him that it was no such thing. He was unconvinced. I have therefore caused you to be placed in an empty cabin in my suite. Is this agreeable to you?"

"It is awfully kind of you," said Stella. "Are you sure I am not in your way?"

"Not in the least. The cabin contained nothing but my heavy luggage, which has now gone to the ship's baggage room. You are very welcome to the cabin. It makes no difference to me."

Silence fell between them; Mr. Li occupying it by examining his finger-nails with even more minute care.

"I could not think of any other arrangement," he said, without looking up. "You would have been ill if you had stopped in that cabin."

"I am exceedingly grateful," said Stella, wondering how much longer the interview was going to drag on in this inconclusive manner.

"You have no need to be, the cabin was standing empty." He looked up suddenly, his eyes wide open this time, and glittering like dark jewels. " I should advise you, however, not to mention to any one that I have placed this state-room at your disposal. It might be misunderstood. You know, I hope, that I have no other wish than to do you a kindness, as one human being to another, but that will not be believed." He suddenly smiled, showing very white teeth between his rather full, colourless lips. " You see, you made an error of judgment when you addressed me as if I were your grandfather."

Stella laughed, and the tension of the interview perceptibly relaxed. "I could not see your face under that lamp in the waiting room, and you talk as if you were an old man."

"That is because I learnt your language from elderly men, and have never had anything to do with young people of your race."

"Not when you were at Oxford?"

"No, I lived out of college with a tutor. The life of an Asiatic in your country is not too pleasant, you know. Your countrymen have developed strong racial prejudices during the last generation, which my grandfather tells me were not present when he came over first."

"I do not share those prejudices," said Stella.

"That is because you are inexperienced. You soon will, when you get out East."

"Why should I?"

"Because it is the custom."

"It is a very stupid custom."

"Not at all, it is a very sound custom. What is it your Poet of Empire said?

'Let the corn be all one sheaf,
And the grapes be all one vine,
Lest our children's teeth be set on edge
With bitter bread and wine.'

"But he also said:

'There is neither East nor West,
Border nor breed nor birth
When two strong men stand face to face,
Though they come from the ends of the earth!'

"Yes, maybe, but not a man and a woman, my child. Now run back to your own quarters," and he held the door open for her.

She scuttled back to the stateroom he had given her, her tail between her legs, feeling very embarrassed, she did not quite know why. Mr. Li seemed to have an extraordinary capacity for making her feel embarrassed. When she had had that long and delightful talk with him in the fog-bound waiting-room, she had had the upper hand, and had forced him to thaw; but now he had recovered the lead and frozen up himself, and frozen her too. She felt chilled to the marrow, and very cheap. She wondered whether he would expect her to keep up the farce of pretending in public that they had never set eyes on each other. It seemed rather foolish to do so, as all the ship's company would probably hear in due course of the ruction over the stateroom.

She saw, however, that Mrs. Cragg's attitude toward the Yellow Peril had not been unique, and a flood of gossip would be let loose if she were seen to be on friendly terms with a China-man. Not that she cared about that. Such prejudices were not only stupid but wicked. Mr. Fook had been a good old man, a true friend in trouble; Mr. Li was charming and cultured, and had shown much more Christian charity than the professed Christians in concerning himself with a little stray orphan who happened to look ill.

But even if she did not care about gossip, apparently he did. Perhaps in his position as a banker it would do him harm. She would take her cue from him and act accordingly.

That night the first of the Biscay swell began to lift them, and Stella was incapable of taking her cue from anything else for the next forty-eight hours.

The stewardess was very attentive, but Stella did not like her as well as her original stewardess, who had been personally kind. She wondered whether she shared the general prejudice against friendly relations between East and West, and rather suspected she did, and that her prejudice was only held in check by the scale on which Mr. Li might be presumed to do his tip-ping.

Stella wondered what form the tail-twisting of the purser had taken. She had guessed during their brief association, that the Chinese valet was terrified of his master, for he skipped like a flea whenever he was addressed. The stewardess was subdued, the valet scared stiff, and the purser had evidently had the fear of God put into him—so it looked as if calm, kind, polite Mr. Li were a Tartar when roused.

Stella neither saw nor heard anything of him or his man servant while she lay in her comfortable bed paying tribute to Neptune. There must be another bathroom, for no one came past her end of the passage save the steward and stewardess. Mr. Li was leaving her severely alone. Neither had she made any friend sufficiently intimate among the passengers for her absence to cause enquiry. No doubt others too had their troubles with Neptune.

The steward brought her a bottle of champagne to help down the cold chicken he was trying in vain to persuade her to eat, announcing that this was the proper treatment for sea-sickness.

Stella looked at it anxiously. I am afraid I can't afford it if it is an extra," she said, doing some hasty mental arithmetic.

"Don't you worry, miss, it won't go down on your bill," the steward reassured her. So she drank it, and found it extraordinarily different from the champagne she had tasted when one of the landlady's daughters had got married.

CHAPTER III

STELLA found, when she returned to the land of the living, that the solemn farce of non-recognition had been modified to the extent of a stiff bow. She took her cue, and inclined her head unsmilingly, averted her eyes, and walked on.

This went on for several days on the comparatively rare occasions when she passed within bowing distance of Mr. Li. It was extraordinary that two people should be within the confined space of ship-board and see each other so seldom. Only at meal-times did she see him, away across the saloon, and as far as she knew, he had never once looked in her direction. She was a little annoyed—*spretae injuria formae*—she was also rather sorry, for he was quite the nicest person on board the other passengers, who had soon begun to make friends with her when they saw that she was travelling alone, were pleasant enough, but there wasn't one that did not bore her, accustomed as she was to the society of men of more than average intellectual calibre for those who follow the call of Empire and its far-flung trade are not often intellectuals

"It is too absurd," thought Stella, "the only person I really like on board this ship is Mr. Li, and I believe the only person he really likes is me, and yet we can't be friends because of this wicked race prejudice."

However, the inevitable boat-drill, very thoroughly practised because of the possibility of torpedoes when they got into Chinese waters, introduced everybody to everybody, and Stella began to get involved in deck games, and an enterprising youth was trying to teach her to dance, though without much success and Mr. Li faded into the background.

Then an incident occurred which brought him into the

foreground of the whole ship. Dinner was proceeding as usual when a sudden hush fell on the dining-saloon as it was heard that voices were being raised in most unparliamentary language at the captain's table. The captain himself was absent, the ship being in soundings, and there was no one to act as host and keep order there. By virtue of his position the purser should have gone over and done so as soon as he heard the trouble starting, but he chose to turn a deaf ear. The doctor was a young man and this was his first voyage and although he looked round anxiously he did not like to take the initiative over the heads of his seniors The old chief engineer, a little hard of hearing, and in any case totally indifferent to his surroundings, went on with his gobbling without realising that trouble was afoot, so the quarrel had time to get going in good earnest before any one tackled it.

The insult of her scorned beauty.

Some hard-boiled Australian, who had had altogether too many pre-dinner cocktails, had taken it into his head to insult Mr. Li; and Mr. Li, his Oxford accent very pronounced, was not taking it lying down, but was giving as good as he got. Stella could not hear what was being said, but saw jaws drop all down the captain's table. Another man joined in, and then another. Mr. Li turned from one to the other with perfect suavity, his voice merely rising a semitone in pitch, but what he was saying seemed to act like vitriol.

Everybody was amazed at the turn things had taken; there did not seem to be anything in the dispute to have started up such serious trouble. It was as if the petty spark of a tipsy man's rudeness had touched off a concealed powder-barrel, and Li was relieving his feelings by letting fly, and a Chinese in a tantrum is a very awkward handful; for just as his control is far greater than a European's, so is his explosion correspondingly greater when the lid finally comes off.

The chief engineer slewed clumsily round in his chair, leaned across to the purser at the parallel table, and murmured in a husky whisper:

"Ye'd better tackle that," jerking his thumb in the direction of the top table to indicate what it was that had to be tackled—as if any one in the crowded saloon could be ignorant of it.

But the purser chose to be as deaf as the adder of Scripture. Ladies were beginning to get up and leave the table, though the dinner was less than half through. The chief engineer leant across a second time, and said in a tone that could not be ignored:

"Will you deal wi' this, Mr. Williams, or shall I?"

The purser rose to his feet none too steadily—it was probable that he too had been cocktailing before dinner with the sozzled nuisance who had started the trouble—strolled across the saloon with his hands in his trouser pockets, and said in a loud voice:

"Mr. Li, I'll trouble you to finish your dinner in your own cabin if you can't behave yourself."

This was a handling of the situation that poured oil on the flames rather than the troubled waters. Li, looking like an angry cat, glared at the purser out of slit eyes.

"No, Mr. Purser," he said," I will not go to my cabin, and you cannot make me."

"I think you'll find I can," said the purser provocatively.

"I think you will find that you cannot," said Mr. Li. "For no one but the captain can order the use of force, and if he orders the use of force, he will not be able to get a single stevedore to handle cargo or coal anywhere on the China coast. Therefore the captain, being a sensible man, will not order force to be used with me; and as you cannot remove me except by force, I shall remain here and finish my meal. Hein? Have you anything to say to that?"

Before the livid purser could answer, the old chief engineer, who had been slewing his best ear round towards the rumpus, rose from his chair and came lumbering across the saloon, interposed a heavy shoulder between the quarrelsome Chinaman and the equally quarrelsome Welshman, drove an elbow that conveyed considerably more than a hint into the waist coat of the latter, and standing over the infuriated Asiatic like an old bull with lowered head, said:

"Mr. Li, sir, I'm an auld mon, and yell respect ma years and mind what I say. The mon that gives heed to the worrds of ony pairson the worse for drink is no better than him. Ye're a sensible mon, and I look to ye to keep the peace wi' fules, for the good Lord himsel' canna cope with them till they're ripe for Hell-fire; an' I gie ye ma worrd as a Christian that's whaure they'll gang."

"Hem?" said Mr. Li. "You are Mr. Macpherson, I think?"

"Ay, ah'm Andra' Macpherson, forty year in China Seas come Michaelmas; and mony's the time yer paw, an' yer gran'paw, too, for the matter o' that, have crossed wi' me. Ye get on wi' yer denner, sir, an' I'll see to it ye're no aifrontit."

The steward tactfully popped a menu in front of Mr. Li, and Mr. Macpherson lumbered off, pushing the purser in front of him.

As he lowered himself into his chair with a grunt his next door neighbour said:

"By Jove, Macpherson, you handled that well. You had the makings of nasty trouble there."

"Ay, the purser laddie didna' ken juist how nasty. He's new to the route."

"I thought the fellow looked like running amok," said the man next to Steila.

"Na, that's Li Wu Lu, he wouldna' do that. He's no need. He could tak' the skin off us by other methods."

"Good Lord, is that Li Wu Lu? That mild-looking chap?"

"Ay, that's him, an' a verra pleasant gentleman too, in the ordinar' way. He's had much provocation to-night, mind ye."

"Something certainly seems to have got him on the raw. You tell that purser of yours, and the fool who started the fuss, not to go ashore in any Chinese port, for they won't come back —not with a whole skin, anyway."

"They'll be nane the waur' for that," said the engineer philosophically, and devoted himself to his food.

Stella lingered over her meal till she saw that Mr. Li had finished and gone, for she had no wish to meet him at that moment. There was something about that fracas that had scared her—a sense of forces of which she had no conception let loose for reasons she did not understand. She did not want to be drawn into any discussion of the affair, so avoiding the lounge, she went out on deck; but the wind was too keen for her thin evening frock, and she ran down to her cabin to get a wrap.

As she was opening the wardrobe she heard a sound behind her, and there, framed in the doorway leading to the bathroom, stood a Chinaman clad in magnificently embroidered robes of the imperial yellow. Every button down the front of the long gown was a large diamond; on every finger of the delicate yellow hands were long jewelled filigree nail guards like talons. On top of the embroidered skull-cap was a glittering ball of brilliants. As he stood, he was worth a king's ransom. She could not think for a moment who it was, the pale, smooth face looked unfamiliar. Then she realised that it was Li with his hair brushed back Chinese fashion. In European garments he was a dignified, distinguished figure, but clad in his magnificent robes he looked like a prince.

"Will you honour me by partaking of tea and sweetmeats in my humble apartment?" said Li in Chinese.

Stella, half hypnotised by this startling and gorgeous apparition, followed him speechlessly through the prosaic European bathroom into the big stateroom. To her amazement it was completely transformed. Magnificent silks hid the European furniture; marvellous scroll-like pictures, half painted and half written, hung on the walls; on the desk a dish of incense smouldered. In the centre of the available floor-space stood a low carved table, some eighteen inches high, on which were arranged exquisite egg-shell china bowls and a quaint angular teapot to match, flanked by shallow dishes on which queer sweetmeats were piled in little pyramids. It was all small and exquisitely dainty, like a doll's tea-set. At either side of the table large cushions lay on the floor.

"You cannot drink tea ceremonially in that dress," said Mr. Li, lapsing into English. "Will you please me by putting this on?" and he handed her a magnificently embroidered emerald green jacket. She did as bid.

"And these in your hair? " he held out to her a morocco leather case in which lay two tortoiseshell hairpins whose large gold knobs lay heavy in the hand as she raised them.

"They go behind the ears—so."

She inserted them as bid in the coil of hair at the nape of her neck. It was as if a spell had been laid on her and she were moving in a dream.

"You cannot sit on these high heels. Take off your shoes. Now make as if you were going to kneel down, and then sit back on your heels. That is the proper attitude for a woman."

He disposed himself cross-legged, however, at the opposite side of the tea-table.

"Did Mr. Fook teach you the tea ceremonial? No Then I will teach you."

Stella, completely bewildered and not a little scared, found herself having as impersonal and straightforward a lesson in Chinese etiquette as she had ever had with Mr. Fook. She did her best to put the recent unpleasantness out of her mind and concentrate on what she was doing. She did not want to behave foolishly and offend Mr. Li; for one thing, because she was deeply grateful to him, and another, because she was genuinely scared of him, she could not have said why.

The lesson did not go too well. Stella did her best to pay attention and carry out the instructions that were given her in the elaborate ritual of the ceremonial tea-drinking, but her wits were astray and her hands not quite steady.

Mr. Li made no comment till the end, and then he said suddenly in English:

"Are you frightened of me, Stella?"

Stella was so taken aback that she could think of no reply.

"Yes, I see you are," said Mr. Li thoughtfully.

"No, I'm not!" said Stella, finding her tongue in her indignation at this aspersion on her courage.

"I am sorry for what happened in the saloon, but it was unavoidable. You think I lost my temper? I did not. It was necessary to make that fuss. Nothing else would have stopped it. Could you hear what was being said?"

33

"No."

"I am glad. The purser had been gossiping."

Stella did not believe his assertion that he had not lost his temper. His English had no longer its idiomatic quality, which, with a man that knew the language as well as he did, meant that he was doing his thinking in his native tongue.

The frank explanation, that made the situation understandable and so robbed it of its incalculable quality, cleared the air amazingly, and Stella relaxed. Even if the explanation were an unpleasant one, it was better than feeling completely out of one's depth.

"I am awfully sorry that you have been let in for rudeness on my account," she said. "But you know, I really don't care two pins. I have always been accustomed to go my own way and pay no attention to what people thought of me."

"Maybe you could do that in London, my child, with your father to protect you; but if I involve you in gossip where you are going, it will be very unpleasant, for I like you, and I do not want to cause you trouble."

"Was that why you cut me dead when I smiled at you the first evening?"

"Yes, Stella, you mustn't smile at me, not in public, anyway," but he smiled at her that quick, peculiarly charming smile of his, that suddenly lit up his impassive face, "Tell me, do you like my room now that it has got all my own things about?"

"I think they are simply too lovely for words. I have never seen such lovely things outside a museum."

"These are such things as are put into museums in your country, little star; but in mine we think they are made for use, and that the soul of a man is richer for using beautiful things." "And these lovely things I am wearing?"

"I am taking those home as presents."

"For your wife?"

"No, for my concubines. My wife died some years ago with her first child, and I have never replaced her."

Stella's face showed her embarrassment.

He smiled. "You do not understand that, do you, little

star?"

"Well, of course, I am English," said Stella, feeling herself getting red.

"And I am Chinese. That explains everything, doesn't it?"

Stella, very embarrassed, feeling that she was blundering tactlessly, said the first thing that came into her head to get away from the awkward situation, and then wished she hadn't. "Did you never replace your wife because you were so fond of her?"

"No, because I wasn't. You see, I have done what would be the equivalent of 'going native' in an Englishman. I came to England too early, and stopped too long without going home, You know what your Poet of Empire—whom I detest—says? 'Who has heard the East a-calling won't never heed naught else' ? You can apply that to me, reversed. That is why I like talking to you, Yan Tai"

"Why do you call me that?"

"It is my Chinese name for you."

"What does it mean?"

"Never mind. I had not meant to call you that to your face. It slipped out. You know my name? Li Wu Lu. You will call me Wu Lu when we are together like this, and I will call you Yan Tai. It is more friendly than Miss Morris and Mr. Li, and I think we are friends, are we not? " and he smiled his peculiarly attractive smile.

"Yes, we are," said Stella, smiling back at him. " I knew that the first minute we met, but you chose to turn your back on me."

"Yes, I turned my back on you," said Li Wu Lu, his eyes narrowing in a face suddenly become impassive.

He leant towards her across the little table.

"Listen, and do not misunderstand me or think I mean to be unkind. I like your friendship, it is very pleasant and we are both lonely. Let us make the most of these few weeks on shipboard. After that, we go our separate ways. It can do no harm, and we shall both enjoy it. What do you say? Will that suit you? I will teach you Chinese etiquette, which you would not learn in the ordinary way. You shall read the classics with me. It will be good for you. Hein? You would like that?"

"Yes," said Stella shyly, " I would like it very much. You know, I was really very hurt when you turned me down."

"Yes, I know that. You have a transparent face, my child, not like our girls. You must learn to control that if you are to have good Chinese manners—and you must learn to control it in your own interest, too, little star."

"I must learn an awful lot of things, I am afraid. You see, my father taught me all sorts of things that one would never learn in the ordinary way; and all sorts of things never came my way that other girls get as a matter of course."

"Yes, I see that. You are book-wise, my child, but you do not know men and things."

"I know some sorts of men rather well, The men kind of my father used to bring home."   "Dusty scholars?"

"Yes, but awfully nice under the dust, once they woke up. And that was my speciality, making them wake up. I could never get on with boys, but I got on with them all right."

"So I perceive. Do you know that I have sworn a very solemn oath never to make a friend of any European?"

"Why did you do that?"

"Because I hate them, Yan Tai."

"Why do you hate them?"

"Because though they have encouraged me to acquire a white man's mind, they will not allow me a white man's life."

"But you have not got a white man's mind, Mr.—Wu Lu."

"Hein? What makes you say that, Stella?"

"It came out so clearly when you were angry. That was why I felt afraid of you for a bit. You were something strange, incalculable, that I could not understand, I had no means of knowing how your mind was working, or how you were taking things, or what you would be likely to do next, or how far you would be liable to go—I didn't know—I knew nothing—and I was just scared of you, that was all."

"But you like me, Yan Tai?"

"Yes, I like you ever so much; and I am not afraid of you

now that the deeper side of you is covered up again."

"Do you know how you seem to me? All surfaces. You do not know—anything, Stella." "Then why do you like me?"

"I like you because you are a curious mixture of woman and man. You have a woman's heart and a man's mind, and I like that. It is a combination that is not met with in my country. With us, women are women. But I like the mixture, Stella. It brings out something in me that had never been brought out before. Has it ever occurred to you that we value our friends, not so much for what they are, as for what they call out in us?"

"Personally I value people for their characters."

"Hein? Do you? You like me, but what do you know about my character? Judged by your civilised Christian standards, I am a very bad man."

"In what way are you a bad man?"

"I have done ever so many murders—God knows how many, I don't. I lost count long ago."

"Do you mean to say you kill people?" gasped the horrified Stella.

"Yes, if they get in my way, by the dozen. But not with my own hands. Oh, no, nothing so crude as that."

"Oh, I'm so glad," cried Stella with a sigh of relief.

"Hein ? You are glad? But why? What is the difference ? I have a regular staff of assassins on my pay-roll. Yu Fu, my man, he has killed several people for me. He knows all about poisons. He has to protect me from them."

"Oh, but why are you telling me this? Do you mean to kill me?"

"No, I have not the slightest intention of killing you, nor of doing you any harm whatever, Yan Tai; but I think it is good for you to know these things because you are all surfaces. It is good for you that you should be told things, for you are just like a baby. If any one is kind to you, you like them. You like me now, because I am giving you sweetmeats; but when I would not look at you, you did not like me, you were angry with me; and yet I was being kind to you, if you had only known enough to know it. But I might as well talk Chinese to your aunt as talk to you like this."

"What a lovely expression—talk Chinese to my aunt, I must remember that. But it is rotten of you to say I only like you because you are giving me sweets. I'm not a—a concubine. I like people for other reasons than for what they give me. If I didn't like them, it wouldn't make any difference what they gave me."

"Hein? You don't like my concubines?"

"I don't know your concubines, so I cannot say whether I like them or not. I don't even know how many you've got."

"I've got eight at the moment, unless any of them have run away while I have been in Europe. But I am always buying new ones and disposing of the old ones."

"You are awful Even if you do these things, why do you tell them to me?"

"Because it is good for you to know them. Concubines are a perfectly respectable institution in my country, just as respectable as parlour-maids in yours, whose position theirs somewhat resembles."

"It doesn't!"

"It does, believe me, little star."

"You really are the limit! What with your concubines and your assassins, I think you are a dangerous person to know."

"On the contrary, I am a singularly safe person to know because I have my safety-valves. Have you ever realised how many curates marry before they are in a position to do so? And why?"

"I know they are always doing it, but I have no idea why, as a breed, they do it. Is there any 'why' to it ? Isn't it just circumstances ? They are badly paid, and fall in love the same as other folk."

"Well, you know your own country folk best, little star. I defer to your wisdom."

"I feel you are pulling my leg."

"Perhaps I am, but never mind."

Then they talked of ships and sealing-wax and cabbages and kings till eight bells sounded for midnight.

Stella went to bed happier and more exhilarated than she had ever been in all her rather drab life. She had had many devoted friends among the elderly scholars who foregathered with her father, but she had never before had a friendship with a man who was young enough or alive enough to have any of that personal magnetism that flows between a man and a woman. She knew Li Wu Lu was a good deal older than herself—he might have been any age between thirty and fifty, that unlined Chinese face told nothing—but he was an extraordinarily alive personality when he put off his mask of Oriental calm, and his liveness made up for any absence of youthfulness there might be.

Stella, who as he had truly said, knew nothing of anything, considered that his maturity was as good as a chaperon. She would, perhaps, have been careful how she dealt with a Chinese youth of her own age, but she rated this middle-aged banker with the scholars she was accustomed to. She had thought of him when she first met him as an old man because of his precision and deliberateness, and the impression stuck, in spite of the unlined face, jet-black hair, and upright carriage. True, his figure had not got the slimness of youth, but he was a lithe and active man, in his full strength, and very much a live wire mentally.

So Stella, who, as he had said, knew nothing of anything, went off to sleep very happily, and dreamt that she and Li Wu Lu were riding on horseback through beautiful country. He was clad in European clothes, but oddly enough she was still wearing the lovely clothes he was taking home as presents for his concubines.

CHAPTER IV

THE next evening, coming as usual to her cabin to fetch her wrap for the deck after dinner, Stella again heard the knock on the bathroom door, and there was Mr. Li in Chinese dress.

"Shall we repeat the tea-ritual?" he said. "The only way to learn Chinese etiquette is to do it over and over again till it is habitual."

And so each evening they did it. And each evening after the pretty ceremony was finished, they talked till midnight. Then, when there was no longer any need to rehearse the tea ceremony because Stella knew it perfectly, Li started to teach her the things that a well-bred Chinese girl ought to know. How to come into the room in the presence of her betters—and there are very few people who are not the betters of a Chinese girl—how to bow, how to sit down, and when to sit down, and above all, the art and language of the fan, which is both semaphore and safety-valve to its wooden faced wielder.

Once or twice motherly females enquired what Stella did with herself every evening. She told them, and truthfully, that she was studying Chinese.

As a matter of fact, Li, being perfectly bi-lingual, slid from one language into the other and back again without realising what he was doing. Stella asked him once:

"Which language do you think in, Wu Lu?"

And he answered: "When I am reasoning, I think in English, and when I am feeling, I think in Chinese."

Impassive as his face was, she could always tell when he was emotionally stirred because the two languages tended to run one into the other, and he spoke English with a Chinese turn of expression, for he would be thinking in one language and translating mentally into the other. She got to know him so well in those weeks that she marvelled how she had ever thought him, or any other Chinese, stolid. True, the face is a mask, but all the rest of a Chinese is eloquent.

But although she soon learnt to gauge the rise and fall of the emotional barometer—and he was as temperamental as an Irishman beneath his celestial stoicism, which is a placidity of manners and philosophy, not of temperament—she never gained the least inkling of the workings of his mind. Hers, she knew, was an open book to him, and he had a disconcerting way of answering the unspoken thoughts which she had intended to keep to herself, but she never learnt to understand him, much as she liked him. She realised more and more clearly the truth of his words when he had said that we like our friends for their effect on us, not for their characters. Once she quoted to him— and made him very angry—another verse of the poem he had already quoted to her:

> "*The Stranger within my gate,*
> *He may be true and kind,*
> *But he does not talk my talk—*
> *I cannot feel his mind.*
> *I see the face and the eyes and the mouth,*
> *But not the soul behind.*"

"Stella, little star!" he had cried, shaken out of his celestial calm and looking like a cat, as he always did when angry. "Can you see nothing but surfaces? Have you no imagination to understand the thing you do not share? Or is everything you have not held in your hand a sealed book to you? No, it is no use talking to you—you are a baby."

"No more use than talking Chinese to your aunt," said Stella, laughing at his indignation.

"Ho!" said Li, recovering his equanimity but still talking chi-chi. "I could talk Chinese to my aunt, but not to your aunt."

"What do you know about my aunt?" laughed Stella. "She may be a first-class Chinese scholar for all you know to the contrary."

Li's expression changed curiously.

"She is not, believe me."

"Do you know her?"

"Yes, I know her. I do business with your uncle."

"Why did you never tell me?"

He hesitated. "I hardly know why I never told you, Yan Tai. Perhaps it seemed to me that this friendship of ours over the teacups was a kind of fairy thing, that would turn to dust, like the jewels bought in the Goblin Market, if one looked at it by daylight. It is a thing that must be kept apart from everyday life, like a fairy story."

"Then I shall see something of you after I land? But you said the Chinese and the English never meet?"

"Yes, and no, Yan Tai. They touch surfaces, as it were. I move a little in European society in the treaty ports because I do much foreign business and it pays me to know how people are feeling and thinking. But there is no intimacy. I go to the club, the racecourse, at-homes, a formal dinner sometimes, but no one is under any delusion that I am a friend of the family."

"But still, I shall see you?"

"Yes, you will see me—in the distance, like it was at first on board this ship. And you must learn to control your face better than you did then, my child, or you will get us both into hot water."

"And like it was on this ship—shall I have tea with you sometimes when no one is looking?"

"Hein, Stella, I don't know. We will see how things go."

"Well, I shall be very disappointed if I don't."

He did not answer.

And so the days went by. Sometimes, when Li meant to go into the smoke-room for a game of chess after he had packed Stella off to bed, he did not change into Chinese dress, and then he did not sit on the cushions—trousers not responding well to such treatment—but on the settee under the porthole with the tea-table between his feet Stella, kneeling on her cushion, felt as if she were worshipping some heathen deity as she looked up into his strangely alien face that never grew familiar however much her friendship with the man might deepen, and there were times when it seemed as if they had drawn very close together.

But although she felt more in harmony with him than she had ever felt with any living being, not excepting her father, to whom she had been devoted, she always had a slight sense of fear at his strangeness, which was accentuated whenever he wore anything characteristically Chinese. In fact she had interdicted the wearing of the nail-guards at the tea-rituals because they affected her so unpleasantly.

"If you had worn a pigtail, I should never have been able to make friends with you," she had told him.

"And if you had had a long, sharp nose, and pale eyes, and frizzy flaxen hair, I should have spared myself the sight of you," he had retorted.

Misfortune had befallen the purser at the first Chinese port at which he had gone ashore. Some one jostled him and he fell in a muck-heap, and a Chinese muck-heap is the quintessence of uncleanliness, treble-distilled. At the second port of call he had the misfortune to collide with one of those individuals whose two nominally—very nominally—covered buckets on the ends of a pole balanced precariously across the shoulders, do for China what the drains and sewers do for Western nations. In fact, whenever the purser went ashore he met with evil-smelling misfortune. .

Stella challenged Li with being the author of his misfortunes, and he folded his hands in his sleeves and looked excessively Oriental, and said:

"Not I, but the gods. He has an impure mind, and it attracts impurity to him."

And then at length, unbelievably, the six weeks that had seemed an eternity when Stella was faced with the prospect of passing them in her terrible first cabin, drew to an end, and Li said to her:

Stella, my child, are you not going to pack, for we land to-morrow?

"Oh yes," said Stella, "I suppose I must. I am afraid I have been putting it off till the last minute."

They rose from where they had been sitting at the little low tea-table, and for a moment they stood face to face silently. Stella saw that Li meant to say something important; she, for her part, had somehow managed to put the inevitable parting out of her mind till it had lost its sense of reality, but suddenly, as he spoke, it smote her full in the face.

"I am going to say good-bye to you now, Yan Tai, for I have no wish to do it in public in the morning. I shall raise my hat and bow then, and you will nod and pass by."

"Oh, say au revoir, not good-bye," cried Stella. "I shall be seeing you from time to time, shan't I ?

"No, you will not. This is the end, Yan Tai. The end for all practical purposes, that is; for such casual meetings as there may be can hardly count as friendship. Now listen, Stella, and play your part as I have taught you. Fold your hands in your sleeves and make obeisance reverently. That is how Chinese maidens behave when they are being sacrificed or the good of their family, or the land, or the Emperor. Our holiday is over. Board-ship friendships, as you very well know, are fleeting, and ours is no exception to the rule. It has been delightful, but now it must end. It cannot be otherwise, for both our sakes. It is good to have known you, Yan Tai, I like you very much indeed.

"Now, child, remember this, for I mean it seriously. If ever you are in trouble, you have a friend in me."

"How shall I find you?" said Stella brokenly, struggling to play her part of stoical Chinese maiden, but unable to control her voice.

"You will have no difficulty in finding me. I am well known. The head office of my bank is next to your uncle's go-down.' A letter there will always reach me sooner or later. Good-bye, Yan Tai." He held out his hand. She placed hers in it. He shook it firmly and unemotionally and let go. " It has been a great pleasure to have known you," he said.

He held open the door of the stateroom for her, and she passed out through the bathroom to her own quarters. There she flung herself face downwards on her bed and wept till she could weep no more.

Consequently she was still engaged in flinging her belongings pell-mell into her cabin-trunk when a steward came to tell her that her aunt had come on board and was asking for her. Hastily sitting on the lid, she got her trunk shut some how and went on deck, heavy-eyed and exhausted from her stormy night, her hair done anyhow and her dress crumpled to a rag from her exertions. She was not calculated to make a good first impression.

She could not remember her aunt, not having seen her since she was little more than a baby, but directed by the steward, she went up to two ladies standing together near the gangway, chatting to the purser, of all people. But the purser's eyes were all round him, like a nervous horse, and Stella felt pretty certain that he was not risking encountering something more solid than Chinese slops.

She went towards them, and the purser faded away when he saw her coming. As she approached she realised that the two ladies were mother and daughter—her Aunt Florence and her cousin Rosemary, but it was not till one got close to them that one realised that they belonged to different generations; for Mrs. Hope had a slender figure, and under the shade of her wide-brimmed hat her heavy make-up looked natural at a little distance. But at close quarters the drastic dieting that had preserved her figure was seen to have taken heavy toll of her face; the skin, delicate pink and white to the unobservant eye, hung in folds like a bloodhound's, and lines of anxiety and irritability about mouth and eyes showed that nerves as well as skin had suffered under the drastic régime.

Rosemary, a buxom, bouncing damsel, good-looking in an obvious kind of way that did not promise much intelligence, stared at her new cousin with frank distaste, Mrs. Hope, more worldly-wise, masked her feelings under a rather hollow cordiality. Stella's heart sank, and her lack of social experience was very much in evidence as she returned their greetings with tepid enthusiasm. Being relations, convention required that they should peck each other's cheeks, but they all looked glad when this duty had been discharged.

They were in a hurry to get off, and Stella had already kept them waiting with her belated packing, so after little more than the bare exchange of greetings, they all got into the large limousine that stood waiting on the quay. Driving out of the dock gates, however, they were held up by an even larger limousine of a very pale dust-like grey, which was itself held up by a broken-down tram.

"Look, Mummy," cried Rosemary, "I do believe that's Mr. Li's car."

Mrs. Hope peered through lorgnettes.

"Yes, I believe it is. Was he on board your boat, do you know, Stella?"

"Yes, I believe he was," said Stella miserably, gazing at the non-committal back of the limousine that held her friend.

Then the tram was pushed clear of the crossing, the grey limousine got quickly away, and with its rapid acceleration left the imposing but elderly Daimler of the Hope family behind.

Arrived at the house that was to be her home indefinitely, Stella felt her heart sink to yet further depths of misery and shyness, for a luncheon party was apparently the order of the day, and the guests had already begun to arrive. None knew better than she that she looked as if she had been sleeping under a hedge, with her tumbled frock and hastily-done hair; and usually neat and dainty in her simple way, no one hated it more than she did.

Cocktails were in progress in the big lounge hall, lunch being already overdue, and as soon as Stella had been presented to her uncle and an assortment of the guests, they adjourned to the table. After the bare introduction, no further notice was taken of Stella by anybody; host and hostess were occupied with their other guests, and Rosemary, who might have looked after her, having other fish to fry in the shape of a couple of young men. Stella sat silently between two not very prepossessing gentlemen who talked across her as the conversation went up and down the table. She knew beyond any shadow of doubt that she was not going to be happy at Esperanza House.

Her mind was far away from the talk that was going on all around her, when through the babble of sound she heard a name that caught her ear.

"Robert," Mrs. Hope called down the table above the din. "Mr. Li was on board Stella's boat."

"Thank goodness for that," said Mr. Hope. "Now I'll be able to get hold of him and get something settled."

"Oh no, you won't," Stella's next-door neighbour called across her. " He's cancelled all appointments and gone straight up country, goodness knows where, and goodness knows why."

"Good God! How long for?" exclaimed Mr. Hope in a tone of utter exasperation.

"Nobody knows. Not even his compradore.' All he knows is that he got a radio last night to cancel all appointments, and no reason given."

"Well, I call it damned discourteous," said Mr. Hope irritably, and a gloom fell on the hitherto animated table. Mrs. Hope did her best to pull her party together with a forced brightness, but the bottom was out of it. Mr. Hope gave her no help, but appeared sunk in gloomy rumination, and his mood was contagious.

Suddenly Stella nearly jumped out of her chair. Behind her the Chinese butler was giving instructions to his assistants in his own language, and although she did not know the meaning of all the expressions he used in referring to his employers, she understood enough to guess their gist. To say that his language was unseemly was to put it mildly. But nobody turned a hair, and Stella realised that of all these men carrying on their business in China, and all these women making their homes there, not one had troubled to learn enough of the language to know that they were being grossly insulted by their own servants to their very faces.

The lunch ran its course. The post-lunch cocktails ran theirs, too, but not before Stella was amazed and horrified to see that quite a proportion of the guests had taken appreciably more than was good for them.

And so the day too ran its course, and Stella found herself in bed toward midnight, very weary and deadly bored.

It was not a happy household. The servants called their employers by every opprobrious epithet to which they could lay their tongues with an air of profoundest humility, and their employers, knowing not a word of the language of their adopted country, were none the wiser. The medium of communication was pidgin, that hideous hybrid in which the vocabulary is English and the construction Chinese. The Hopes were not well served, partly because the service was sullen and unwilling, and partly because very frequently the servants genuinely did not grasp what was required of them.

The amah, in particular, was stupidity personified. Stella formed the opinion that she was half-witted, and wondered why they employed her. She gathered, however, that all amahs were the same, and that nothing was to be gained by changing her. She knew her routine duties and went through them like an automaton, and a new amah would have to be broken in, a most laborious process when neither party spoke the other's language; so they preferred the devil they knew to the devil they didn't.

In bed at night, quiet after the endless petty distractions of that restless household, Stella used to live over again the days of her brief friendship with the Chinese banker. They had been the happiest days she had ever known in her rather drab life. She admitted to herself quite frankly that he had attracted her tremendously; but she admitted to herself equally frankly that the situation was an impossible one, even if he had felt towards her as she had felt towards him, and she had no reason to believe that he did. There had never been one word, one hint, one look of love-making. He had shown her kindness, but it was kindness that cost him nothing save the kindly thought; he had frankly enjoyed her company, but had equally frankly told her that it was a board-ship friendship that would end with the

48

voyage. Any one who charged Mr. Li with sentimentality, let alone any thing in the way of an abduction or seduction, was just romancing.

Stella knew it perfectly well—had never known anything better—and yet her matter-of-fact association with the Chinese banker had awakened first love in her heart, and first love is a very strong thing.

Stella's life ever since she had left her not very pleasant school had been a lonely and frustrated one. Money was scant, and it never entered her father's head that what suited him might not suit her. He was perfectly content to spend his days in the Museum reading-room, and to take a walk in Regent's Park on a Sunday when the reading-room was shut. He loathed the pictures, did not care for music, and could not afford theatres. His annual birthday present to his daughter from the age of twelve was a library subscription; on her sixteenth birthday he gave her a wireless set with headphones, so that she could listen in without disturbing him. She made tea for, and listened to the talk of, his scholastic friends, and when she felt the need of air and exercise, went for walks by herself. For their annual holiday they went to the seaside, it is true, but put up in rooms because her father disliked the enforced sociability of a boarding-house; they went for walks together on the promenade, and sat together on the pier listening to the band. She had never had any enlightenment upon life and its problems save from the crude, and sometimes coarse, philosophy of landladies.

But Stella was no fool, and had been trained in a Spartan tradition of self-control; she accepted the situation with the stoicism of the sacrificed Chinese maiden she had been bidden to emulate. Save for that one night of weeping over her stillborn love, she shed no more tears. Nevertheless, when various men, more or less attractive— Rosemary having picked them over first and attached to herself anything worth having—were trotted up and down, as it were, in her presence, Stella remained utterly unresponsive. She had known, in her brief weeks of friendship with Li Wu Lu, hopeless as it all was, something of what was possible between a man and a woman, and a marriage of convenience was not for her.

Mrs. Hope was furious. This was an eventuality she had never reckoned with when she had invited her sister's child to make her home with her. She had reckoned upon presiding over a pretty wedding within the year. To have an unmarried niece settling down into old-maidhood on her hands was a prospect she had never bargained for, When she was slimming her temper was short and her patience scanty, and she spoke her mind exceedingly plainly. She challenged Stella with cherishing a hopeless love-affair, which Stella, being a respecter of the truth, did not deny; rigorous questioning elicited the fact that it was for a man much older than herself who had not the slightest intention of getting himself involved with her. Mrs. Hope, having heard no breath of scandal from friends who had travelled by the same boat as Stella—thanks to the precautions observed by Mr. Li—naturally jumped to the conclusion that the unresponsive lover had been left safely behind in England, and that time could be relied on for an early cure.

But as the weeks, and then the months went by, and there was no sign of improvement, she began to despair. Stella did not ride, did not dance, did not play bridge, did not play tennis, had no small talk, and showed little aptitude for acquiring these accomplishments, for they did not interest her. Despite the fact that she was in the midst of the gayest of social whirls, Stella remained as solitary as if she were marooned on a desert island, as in fact she was, so far as any human sympathy was concerned; for she had not a single idea or aim in common with those who surrounded her. No one attempted to find out what she was interested in; no one attempted to draw her out. It was a problem in maladaptation and the survival of the unfit that would have baffled Darwin himself. In the household of her aunt, Stella had much the same effect as a bit of grit in the eye. It was a problem for both parties.

When she arrived, her scanty wardrobe had been completely overhauled and liberally supplemented with Rosemary's cast-offs, but these neither suited nor fitted her. Rosemary was a rosy-cheeked, blue-eyed, big-boned blonde; Stella was a black-haired, daintily-made, creamy-skinned brunette. However skil-fully the old amah might alter and make over, the result was a foregone conclusion. Nevertheless, Stella had to put up with it, for Mrs. Hope was on the economical tack, Mr. Hope's affairs being none too prosperous at the moment.

Compelled to wear unbecoming clothes, and knowing that every one knew them for cast-offs, Stella lost all interest in her appearance; her madonna-like head, borne like a flower on its graceful neck, stuck incongruously out of the frills and furbe-lows; the pale bright colours, that set off Rosemary's pink and white, making her creamy skin look sallow, Discerning people, had there been any in the set of which Mrs. Hope was the cen-tre, would have known that Stella's careless dress was as symp-tomatic as the staring coat of a horse.

Gradually Stella sank into apathy. Her father's death left a great gap in her life after the years of close companionship wherein as she grew older she had taken to a great extent the place of her dead mother; her first love affair had collapsed ignominiously, or perhaps to say that it had died stillborn would be a better expression; and she could strike no roots in the utterly unsympathetic soil to which she had been transplanted, and like a transplanted plant, she drooped and withered. As her cheeks grew whiter and thinner, her dark eyes looked big-ger and darker, and she slipped silently through the crowded rooms of Esperanza House like a little white ghost. The sport-ing, hard-drinking, money-worshipping crowd that frequented those rooms accepted her presence nonchalantly and paid no attention to her.

One use, and one use only was found for her—Mrs. Hope was a very nervous motorist and Chinese chauffeurs did not inspire her with confidence. Rosemary had learnt to drive, but she was an exceedingly slap-dash young woman, and her moth-er soon realised that whatever confidence she had had in her daughter was more than misplaced; so she tried out Stella, and Stella, being steady and careful, gave satisfaction. Consequently she got all the driving to do, and many a bored hour did she pass, yawning at a dance or watching her aunt play bridge, till

51

such time as the scattered family was ready to be collected and taken home. No one troubled to look beneath her unresponsive exterior and make friends with her; it was just accepted as a matter of course that there should be an unattractive niece hanging about in the background at Esperanza House; she was as unconsidered as the cat.

She heard Mr. Li's name mentioned fairly frequently, for he bulked big in the world of Chinese commerce that her uncle and his friends moved in. His disappearance up country appeared to cause a great deal of inconvenience; it seemed as if no deal could be put through, no contract settled, without at least his good will. Mr. Hope was particularly disgruntled because the lease of his dock and warehouse had run out, and Li was his landlord, and he did not know upon what terms he could get it renewed. He had been inspecting various other properties along the water-front in search of alternative accommodation should Li prove too grasping, but apparently the Chinese banker had been buying up all available water-front property for years, and all roads led back to him.

Stella heard the subject discussed at the dinner-table, and saw the men forget their social manners and go into it as if in a board-room.

"It's a dashed good job for you you've always kept on friendly terms with him, Hope," said one of the men, "Li has a reputation for tail-twisting when he's offended."

Stella, remembering the purser's unsavoury accidents, believed him.

"What's your candid opinion of Li, McCulloch—as a fellow banker? You've had more to do with him than any of us."

A man with a short grey beard, who had not uttered a word throughout the meal, sat in silent thought for a moment.

"I have always found Li Wu Lu absolutely straight," he said. "His word is his bond, but of course he has Chinese notions of vengeance. He is certainly far and away the most influential man in this part of the world, owing to his hold on the Tongs."

"What in the world does he do with tongs?" exclaimed the

newly arrived bride of a junior partner.

"Tongs, my dear lady," said the grey-bearded banker, "have other uses than putting on coal in China. They are a cross between trade unions and secret societies, and are the only stable things left in Chinese life to-day, thanks to Communism and modernism and the end-results of three thousand years of Chinese education and officialdom. Li Wu Lu has set to work and organised the Tongs in this province into a federation of which he is the president; it is rumoured that he aims at extending his federation throughout all China in order to resist Japanese influence, and his trip inland at the present moment points in that direction. If he could, it would save the country from anarchy and probably hold back the Japanese for another generation."

"We don't want the situation cleared up just yet," said Mr. Hope, "we are doing very well as we are."

"It is a terrible thing to see a civilisation collapse," said the banker.

"Plenty of pickings," said Mr. Hope.

Mr. McCulloch looked at him sharply, stroked his beard, and said nothing.

CHAPTER V

THREE months had passed slowly by. It had been the night of the new moon when Stella had landed, and she had been kept awake for the better part of it by the celebrations that were being carried on in the Chinese quarter in its honour; and now, for the third time, the process had been repeated, and she and the rest of the household had had their sleep disturbed by the Chinese idea of music, and nerves were taut and tempers short in consequence.

She had driven her aunt and cousin and a party of bright young people out to the racecourse, where the pony races, which took place as a weekly institution, had long ceased to have the slightest interest for her unless the ponies were naughty; she was sitting in the car sewing, leaving other folk to amuse themselves in the paddock, when a feeling that she was being watched made her look up, and there was Mr. Li, clad in a very smart white linen suit, leaning on the door of the car and gazing steadily at her out of his narrow, inscrutable eyes. A sudden breathlessness took her, and a roaring in the ears, and a darkness before the eyes. Then it mercifully cleared, and she heard him say:

"Hein, Stella, I thought you were going to faint!"

"No, I wasn't," said she. "I've never fainted in my life. I am just a bit run down. I don't think this place suits me."

"The place—or the people?" said Li.

Stella looked at him.

"Did you know what it was going to be like?" said she.

"I knew, yes. But it was no use to prejudice you by telling you. Better to let you make the best start you could. You might have liked it. How did I know? They are your people, not mine.

54

There is plenty of amusement; very good food; no work. Hein. You might like it, Stella. How did I know?"

Stella looked at him, but it was impossible to tell from his expressionless face whether he was sincere or sarcastic.

"Do you know what the servants call my aunt's house?" she said.

"No? What do they call it?"

"They call it the House where the Rice is Bitter."

"Hein," said Li, noncommittally. "Good afternoon, Miss Morris. I am sorry you are not enjoying your visit to China," and he raised his hat and turned away, disappearing amid the tangle of parked cars as 'God save the King' from the bandstand announced that the afternoon's sport was over. Stella folded her sewing with shaking hands and pushed it into the pocket in the door of the car where she kept it to beguile such weary hours of waiting as this, while other folk amused themselves with pastimes in which she had no share; and knowing the habits of the elderly car, she got out to wind the starting-handle so that there should be no delay when the family party arrived. But before she could touch it a smartly uniformed Chinese chauffeur stepped forward, saluted, took the starting-handle from her, started up the car, saluted again and vanished. Stella, staring startled after his retreating back, saw a big, dust-grey limousine parked just behind the Daimler.

In a few moments she heard the shrill chatter approaching that always seemed to hang round her aunt and cousin like fog round an iceberg, and the family party hove in view. Stella got back into the driving-seat, and waited apathetically for them to sort themselves and their belongings, staring out into space over the dusty plain where the ponies had been disporting themselves.

Suddenly the cackle rose crescendo, and Stella, looking round to see who was being welcomed with acclamation, saw Mr. Li bowing over her aunt's hand in a most gallant manner that evidently greatly delighted that lady; then he repeated the process with Rosemary, despite her obvious embarrassment at the formality. Of herself he took not the remotest notice; she might have been completely non-existent though she was sitting within a yard of him; but she was used to this manoeuvre of his, and sat watching him as indifferently as if she had never set eyes on him before.

She listened to the amiable social nothings that were being exchanged, and wondered what her aunt would have thought if she had heard Mr. Li when he lost his temper with the purser. It would certainly have been an eye-opener for any one who only knew the Chinese banker as his polite and polished social self. She thought of Bret Harte's poem about his namesake at Poker Flat, and smiled inwardly. Mr. Li was just as childlike and bland as that other Li, and she wondered whether he too had a few aces up his sleeve.

The other cars were starting up and driving away, but Mr. Li showed no disposition to move, and stood calmly discussing Chinese art with her aunt, who was something of a collector in a spasmodic and undiscerning way. Rosemary showed obvious signs of wanting to be off, but her mother ignored them and seemed perfectly prepared to stand gossiping with Mr. Li as long as he was prepared to stand gossiping with her.

Stella heard him recommending some shop in the Chinese part of the town as a marvellous place for the bargain-hunter.

"The only drawback is that Mr. Wang does not speak a word of English," he was saying. "Now if you had only honoured us by learning our language, Mrs. Hope—"

"Oh, that does not matter, my niece speaks Chinese quite well. She can do the bargaining."

Stella, rather startled, not knowing quite what was pending, wondered whether an ace had come out of Mr. Li's sleeve.

Bowing, he took his leave without a single glance in her direction, and they all packed into the car and she drove them home. Several times in the course of the drive, however, she earned her aunt's admonition for the erratic way she was handling the car. As she drove, she heard Rosemary also being admonished.

"Rosemary, you must not giggle when Mr. Li bows to you.,,

"I can't help it. He's so funny."

"You wouldn't think he was funny if you were in your father's shoes."

"I can't stick Chinks."

"You've got to stick this one."

Mrs. Hope was not long in availing herself of the information concerning the bargain-hunter's paradise in the lower town, and Stella had to drive the big car as far as it would go down the narrow streets, and then leave it under the care of some exceedingly unsavoury looking ruffians who were soldiers, police or bandits as the case might require, and who appeared to be collecting either tolls or blackmail at the gate of the native quarter, where the Concession ended and Chinese soil began, if that term could properly be applied to the age-old layer of trodden garbage underfoot.

Amid the assortment of odours of that ancient civilisation, some fetid, some aromatic, they continued their way on foot as best they might, watched from the shadows of the low fronted shops by innumerable eyes, curious and unfriendly.

For all her liking for the Chinese, Stella began to feel a little scared. All the same, no one shouted abuse; no one jostled them; no one even begged from them.

Fortunately for them, it was not difficult to find their way, for though the street twisted, they only had to follow it as it wound down the steep pitch towards the harbour. It got steeper and steeper as they went on, till finally they arrived at their destination, where the curio-dealer's shop clung like a swallow's nest to the cliff, with below it a sheer drop to the water-level, very sketchily fenced.

"Good gracious me, where are we?" exclaimed Mrs. Hope. "Why, there's the roof of your uncle's go-down!" and looking straight beneath her, Stella saw a red-roofed shed bearing in large white letters the words: 'Hope Navigation Co.' Her eyes, however, were on its neighbour, a big block of substantial granite buildings whose façade bore in letters of more modest dimensions the words: 'Inland and Overseas Commercial Bank of China and a similar legend in Chinese characters vertically down one corner.

Having got her bearings, for she had entirely lost all sense of direction in the winding Chinese streets, and had not the faintest idea she was so near the harbour, Mrs. Hope led the way, like a ship in full sail, into the emporium whose door stood darkly open on to the street, and whose pine-end was a continuation of the sheer precipice in which the spur of the hills where the town was built broke down in a combe to the harbour.

Unable to see anything in the aromatic darkness after the glare of the street, Mrs. Hope gave the call that summons rickshaw boys, coolies, and such-like small deer, and there rose under her elbow from a low desk at which he had been seated, a small and ancient Chinaman, neatly clad in dark blue silk of the very best quality, with spotless white wristbands of finest linen showing under his wide sleeves. Large horn-rimmed spectacles framed his bright dark eyes and gave an impressive air of learning to his calm, refined, scholar's face, as he stood bowing with serene dignity to the woman who had called him as if he were a coolie. Around him, not in crowded profusion but most artistically displayed, stood the finest flower of China's arts and crafts, every single object a museum specimen. Even Mrs. Hope realised that she had made a mistake in giving that coolie call.

"Oh—er—good afternoon," she said, making such amends as were in her power. Mr. Wang bowed and returned the corresponding greeting in Chinese.

Mrs. Hope turned to Stella.

"Tell him I want to look at his things," she said. But Stella had been better trained than that, and made the customary politenesses in ample form. Mr. Wang beamed his approval and responded in kind.

"What is he saying?" asked Mrs. Hope impatiently.

"He hasn't said anything yet," said Stella. "We're just doing the polite."

"Well, hurry up about it," said Mrs. Hope, turning away to examine the treasures by which she found herself surrounded.

The old gentleman took not the slightest notice of her, but concentrated all his attention and smiles on Stella, and fairly spread himself. It was a royal reception. Stella had never suspected that such an elaboration of flattery was possible. She did her best to reply in kind, but was hopelessly outdistanced in the politeness race, the old man getting in three compliments to her one.

Presently the spate of politeness showed signs of slackening, and Stella led Mr. Wang gently into the paths of business, and he turned towards Mrs. Hope, and with a rather cursory bow, as if he realised that politeness was wasted on her, began to display his stock. There was only one question Mrs. Hope asked about anything—" How much?"

When Stella translated the prices that were being asked, Mrs. Hope's eyes grew round with amazement. She did not know much about Chinese objets d'art, but she knew enough to know that these prices were exceedingly moderate. She closed with bargain after bargain, hardly examining it, and Stella, who had repeatedly heard her uncle demanding economy in his household, stood amazed, wondering whether it was her duty to suggest caution. Mrs. Hope noted her startled expression.

"My dear! " she said in a whisper, as if Mr. Wang might understand if she spoke out loud, " we shall never get bargains like this again."

Finally she stopped, more for want of breath than want of money, and wrote out a cheque. Mr. Wang caused her purchases to be loaded onto a hand-cart, and as he bowed her off the premises, pressed into Stella's hand a small parcel.

"What is it ?" she exclaimed, startled.

"Your commission," said Mr. Wang.

"Oh, but I can't accept a commission," cried Stella.

"It is the custom," said the art dealer, retreating into his shop before she could return the package to him.

"What were you two wrangling about?" demanded Mrs. Hope as they made their way back through the narrow streets, as unmolested as they had come. Stella told her. She was immensely amused.

"Do let us look at your commission, Stella," she exclaimed as soon as they were seated in the car, before Stella had even had time to start the engine.

Stella undid the little package in its elaborate wrappings that added so much to the grace of the gift, and in her hand lay a superb necklet of pale jade, its heavy, slightly irregular beads, with their curious, soapy texture, separated one from another by small crystals.

"My dear! How perfectly lovely," exclaimed Mrs. Hope, eying it enviously. "Of course it would not suit Rosemary, but it will suit you to perfection."

Stella wondered whether, if it had suited Rosemary, she would have been called upon to give it up.

Arrived home with their treasures, there was an instantaneous uproar from Mr. Hope when he saw how much money had been spent.

"Don't worry about it, my dear," said Mrs. Hope, "I have not bought all these to keep; they're to sell again; and I shall make the most colossal profit, for I've got the most marvellous bargains."

Among those who dropped in at the cocktail hour, for the Hopes kept practically open house, was a man with a considerable local reputation as a connoisseur; a collector he was not, for being the editor of the local paper, he could not afford to be; but his opinion was in great demand throughout the Concession, and a considerable portion of his income came from the commission on deals.

The bargains were shown him, and he professed himself amazed at Mrs. Hope's good fortune, and announced his intention of visiting Mr. Wang forthwith on his own account.

"You must let Stella take you if you do," said Mrs. Hope, "and then she will pick up her commission on the deal."

"So you collected your rake-off, did you, Miss Stella? You must be an excellent business woman for one so young."

"I did not collect it," said Stella. "It was forced on me."

"Still more marvellous. Do let me see your commission. This old boy really is a rara avis. The last surviving specimen of the old China. If you can spare the time to-morrow morning, we will pay him a call."

So next morning the trip to the Chinese town was repeated. They passed down unmolested. Stella did the negotiating with the amiable and obliging Mr. Wang, and they returned as peacefully as they had come.

Mr. Mathers was silent and preoccupied during the walk back through the narrow streets. Not until they had passed out through the mud gateway did he speak.

"I don't understand the situation at all," he said. "We ought to have passed through a barrage of insults. The goods were priced at much less than their market value, and the necklace you got as your commission is a pretty valuable present. I'll come back and have a word with your uncle."

Mr. Hope was not in when he returned, so he had to content himself with a word with her aunt.

But Mrs. Hope merely gave her habitual giggle.

"We went there on Mr. Li's introduction," she said. "He's a great friend of ours, you know."

"That explains it," said Mr. Mathers. " Wang was trying to conciliate Li by doing the polite to you. You're dashed lucky, Mrs. Hope, or rather Robert is, to be in with Mr. Li like that. He's a curious bird. Make the most of the friendship. It may come in very handy for the Hope Navigation Co."

To Stella's mind there came the memory of the words she had heard over the tea-bowls on board the liner— "I have sworn never to make a friend of a European; I hate them—."

"I expect he thought Stella was Rosemary," she heard Mrs. Hope saying, "and that was why he gave her such a handsome present."

"Yes, I expect he did. I was rather puzzled by that necklet. It's a valuable thing."

They turned to examine Mrs. Hope's bargains, which were now displayed all round the room.

"I say, look here!" exclaimed Mr. Mathers, picking up one of a pair of Ming vases. "This is a do. The other one's genuine, but this one's a fake."

"Good gracious, you don't say so? Yes, I can see the difference now it is pointed out. Stella, you must take these round to-morrow and ask for the money back."

"You mustn't send her down there alone, Mrs. Hope, it isn't safe."

"Yes, it is. It's perfectly safe. They treat us as if we were royalty. Robert's got a tremendous prestige among them, you know, thanks to his friendship with Li."

"Well, I wouldn't send a girl down that slum alone, I can tell you that. And I wouldn't trust Li any further than I could see him, either."

"McCulloch says he's absolutely straight."

"So he is, financially. It's his friendship I wouldn't trust too much if I were you."

"Why ever not? We've known him for years."

"Well, it's no business of mine. I expect Robert can take care of himself. But for God's sake don't send that child down that slum by herself."

Nevertheless next afternoon Mrs. Hope bade Stella go back with the vases.

Nervously clutching her parcel, Stella got out of the tram at the terminus and advanced towards the sinister mud archway and its villainous guard. Amiable grins, however, though they did not add to their beauty, decorated their faces. Stella exchanged the compliments of the season with them in due form, instinctively using the grandee's mode towards them, as she had been taught by Mr. Li, rather than the more commonplace form of address that she had learned from old Fook, and they made the appropriate replies as if it were a matter of course. There was plenty of curiosity during her progress down the street, but no impoliteness. She felt rather like the squire's wife visiting the village.

Old Wang greeted her as if she were his favourite daughter. He professed himself covered with confusion that such a thing should have happened in his shop as the passing of a spurious objet d'art, and explained that they had hardly left the premises when he had discovered the mistake, which was an error of the packer's, those vases having been expressly set aside in the packing room to be returned to the person from whom they had come. He showed her a pair of vases which he said were the ones that had actually been chosen by Mrs. Hope, and she saw that they bore a sufficiently close resemblance to the faulty pair to allow of a perfectly genuine mistake being made by a stupid packer.

Nevertheless, she had the feeling that Wang was up to tricks. The thing that troubled her in dealing with the Chinese, much as she liked them, was that she could not tell when they were sincere or not, or when they were telling the truth or not, and she remembered the words of Kipling's poem that had made Li so angry— 'I can see the face and the eyes and the mouth, but not the mind behind,' and she felt troubled; she liked this old man so much, and yet there was no real contact between them.

She had learnt one thing, however, during her brief but intimate friendship with Li, that it is possible to startle the truth out of a Chinaman, or at least a reaction that gives a clue to the truth, by suddenly shooting a question at him point blank, and she played this trick on Mr. Wang.

"How is it that a foreigner can walk these streets in peace, honourable and learned one?"

But Mr. Wang never turned a hair; in fact he seemed quite prepared for the question.

"That, honourable and noble virgin, is because it is to my great profit to do business with foreigners direct, instead of selling to the middlemen and dealers as I have had to do hitherto, owing to my lack of knowledge of the language and absence of European connections; and when news was conveyed to me from a very honoured and influential source that I might receive a visit from English ladies I requested persons with influence in this district that there should be no impoliteness to my customers, and they have most courteously acceded to my request. Rest assured that you can come and go in perfect safety."

It was a very reasonable explanation, and Stella accepted it.

Mr. Wang caused the offending vase to be smashed before her eyes and made the pieces into a neat parcel which he placed inside one of the pair of genuine vases Then he produced another little package, opened it, and revealed a necklet of the most perfect lapis lazuli.

"A bargain," he said, blinking like a lizard behind his homers. "A very especial bargain, such as does not come twice in a lifetime. I am exceedingly desirous that my esteemed client, your venerable aunt, should see it before it is shown to any one else. Look, I will place it inside this other vase, and if it does not please, she has but to send it back, and if it pleases, she can pay at her convenience."

Stella did not demur. Why should she? The necklet was as Mr. Wang had truly said, a remarkable bargain; it was also exactly the thing for Rosemary, who had openly envied her her jade; true, it meant that if she charged herself with the errand, she would have to return the following day to bring back either the goods or the money, but what did that matter? She was satisfied that she would pass unmolested by the local riff-raff be-cause the local Tong, of which Mr. Wang was certainly a mem-ber, and probably an influential member, had given instructions that the curio-dealer's customers were not to be meddled with. So with due humility she undertook to take the lapis necklace 'on appro': and bring it back if not purchased, inwardly smiling as she did so as she wondered how her aunt would have liked the epithet applied to her in all politeness by Mr. Wang.

But Mr. Wang had not done with her yet. From under a bench he produced a length of heavy dark silk of that red which is produced when mulberry juice is blended with alkalis, and held it up against her face, considering the effect with concen-trated attention.

"Too dark," he said, and put it aside and brought out an-other of the shade of Chinese lacquer.

"That is better," said he, and began to wrap it up in a piece of soft grey paper that contrasted fascinatingly with its rich hue as he turned it about in his delicate artist's hands in the fold-ing.

"Your commission on the vases," he said, laying it in her arms as if it were a baby.

"Oh, but I can't. I really can't. It is not our—our custom," cried Stella, trying to give it back to him; but he pushed it back into her arms and would have none of it.

"And tomorrow, if the venerable aunt buys the necklace, there will be another little commission."

Then, paying no attention whatever to her protests, he invited her to inspect his stock with him, and began to show her this thing, and that thing, explaining their history and, pointing out their beauties and defects; giving her, in fact an exceedingly scholarly lecture on the history and technique of Chinese art, illustrated by examples that no museum could better and few could equal. Stella, absorbed and oblivious, still nursing the disputed silk, lost all account of the time. It was not until the fading light aroused her to its passage that she set off hurriedly over the cobbles in order to reach the gate of the native city before it shut at dusk.

Needless to say, the necklace was received with rapture by Rosemary, and indeed its rich pure intensity of blue set off her cornflower eyes to perfection.

"Oh, Mummy, I must have it! It's absolutely 'me,'" she cried.

"Well, I can't give it you, my dear," said her mother, who was still smarting after a stormy passage concerning the cost of the previous consignment of goods from Mr. Wang. "You will have to buy it out of your allowance."

"All right, I will. He'll give me tick, I suppose, Stella?"

"I don't know. That's for him to say," said Stella, who knew her cousin's financial habits. "I've got to take it back tomorrow, or take the money."

"But he knows it's for us. He'll give us tick," cried Rosemary. Stella, who had thought privately that Mr. Wang had been exceedingly rash in offering to give even her aunt tick, shook her head firmly and held on to the necklace in a way that permitted of no argument.

Rosemary seized her hand, and by squeezing her knuckles, tried to make her loose her hold. Stella set her teeth to endure the pain and hung on grimly. Rosemary began dig to her nails in as well as squeeze; it was a real schoolgirl scramble, and Stella resorted to schoolgirl tactics and kicked her cousin's shins. Rosemary retaliated by smacking her face.

"Children, children ! " cried Mrs. Hope. " Stop! Stop it at once! How dare you behave like this!"

They fell apart Stella opened her hand and the lapis beads rattled on the floor, for the string of the necklace had been burst by the pressure.

"There now, you've been and gone and done it," said Rosemary angrily, and flounced out of the room. Mrs. Hope turned back to her writing-table, taking no further notice, and Stella laboriously picked up the lapis beads one by one, only to find, for all her hunting, she was one short of the number.

Next morning a very subdued Stella presented herself at Mr. Wang's emporium, with the broken necklace in its crushed case in her hands, and explained with abject apologies that it had been accidentally broken and a bead irretrievably lost, which loss she was prepared to make good if Mr. Wang would tell her what it amounted to.

Mr. Wang peered at the crushed case through his horners; then he turned his attention to the bruised and swollen fingers that held it; and then looked Stella straight in the eyes, under one of which a faint dark shadow showed.

"So?" said he. "The House where the Rice is Bitter?"

Stella nodded, unable to speak.

"Chk, chk, chk," said he. "We will drink tea."

He led her out into a tiny room behind the shop, furnished with a low divan, a little tea-table with its accompanying cushions, and an exquisite cabinet. This latter he opened, and took thence a small canister. At his call a youth came from the back of the shop, to him the canister was entrusted, and in a few minutes there appeared a tray with the tea bowls, and the little canister was handed back to Mr. Wang to be locked up in the cabinet again. Then, for the first time in her life, Stella tasted real China tea.

Marvelously restored to peace of mind by that surprisingly potent beverage, Stella, in response to the old man's gentle questionings, told of her position in her aunt's house hold, her loneliness, and her humiliation.

"But you will soon marry and leave it, honourable virgin," said the old man, blinking sagely at her behind his glasses. Stella felt herself getting pink. She shook her head.

"I shall not marry," she said, "I do not like young men and they do not like me. I mean to try and earn my living."

"And how do you propose to do that, if it is permitted to enquire?"

"I have thought that my knowledge of your honourable language might in some way be turned to account."

"It might, it might," said the old man, evidently giving the matter serious thought, "and likewise your natural taste for artistic objects. Honourable virgin, if you seriously contemplate embarking on a commercial career, I beg you to give me the first refusal of your services."

"But—but what work could I do for you? Do you mean it seriously?"

"I mean it exceedingly seriously. You can do for me what you have already done—bring me customers and interpret for me. If you will do this, I will pay you a good commission."

"But—I know nothing about the work."

"I will teach you, and I prophesy that you will be an apt pupil. At least I know that I can trust you," and he gently touched her bruised hand and the beginnings of a slight black eye that showed through her creamy skin.

CHAPTER VI

STELLA returned to Esperanza House in some trepidation. She wondered how her aunt would take the news that she had had a business offer from Mr. Wang. To her surprise that lady took it much better than might have been expected. To be perfectly candid, it looked like solving a problem for her... the problem of Stella sinking into soured old-maidhood on her hands. Not only did she readily agree to Stella's working for Mr. Wang, but suggested she should undertake the peddling of some of the indiscriminate purchases that had not only collapsed Mrs. Hope's personal allowance but also the housekeeping money, and rang up a number of her acquaintances to tell them that Stella had taken on a job with a most delightful old curio-dealer and had the most marvellous bargains to offer, and pushed Stella and her parcels into the Daimler to go round and offer them forthwith.

Stella had not the faintest idea what she ought to ask for the goods with which she found herself thus hastily stocked up, but thought she could not go far wrong if she added fifty per cent, to what her aunt had given for them. This she did, until she realised from the delighted faces of her customers that her mistake had been in adding too little. After that she added a hundred per cent. Peace was more than restored at Esperanza House, and Mrs. Hope sent her out again straight away, to go back to Mr. Wang and purchase the lapis necklace for Rosemary.

It was late when Stella arrived at the gate of the native quarter, and the sky already glowed pink with the sunset. She thought she had plenty of time for her errand, however, for it was only about ten minutes' walk from the gate to Mr. Wang's shop. But she had-reckoned without the latitude, and the dusk fell with southern suddenness and it was almost dark before she reached the end of the narrow winding lane that served as High Street to that rabbit-warren, and the lights were a-twinkle over the water as she reached Mr. Wang's door and found to her horror that it was shut. Not a light showed in all that tall, windowless building, and Stella faced with terror the prospect of a return journey through the winding alleys in the moonless dark if she could not make Mr. Wang hear, and get him to send a shop-boy to see her home.

She began to knock on the heavy barred door with her knuckles; then, finding she was making little impression on its massive timbers, took off her shoe and began to beat upon it with the heel. Heads came out of doors all down the alley at the shindy, but poor Stella took no notice, but beat desperately upon the unresponsive wood.

Across the way a door opened and a man came quietly up beside her, took the shoe from her hand, beat upon the door with a peculiar rhythm, handed her back her shoe, and disappeared into the shadows as quietly as he had come. Stella heard the creak of a board in the dark, silent house, and the door opened half an inch with the faint chain clank of the that held it.

"Wait," said Mr. Wang's voice in a whisper that was little more than a breathing, the door closed as silently as it had opened, and she heard the board creak again as he retreated into the inner parts of the house.

The wait seemed interminable, and Stella grew more and more panic-stricken as she waited. It was pitch dark now, not a crack of light showed from any of the houses that turned windowless faces to the street. Then at last she heard the warning creak of the board again, the door opened soundlessly, and a hand touched hers and drew her into the warm scented darkness of the unlit shop.

A line of dim light showed around the curtain that hid the little inner room from the eyes of customers, and Stella, trembling in every limb, suffered herself to be led silently towards it over the uneven floor. The curtain was drawn back by the claw-like hand of Mr. Wang, and Stella stepped through the archway to find herself face to face with Li Wu Lu, clad in the conventional dinner-jacket of civilisation, seated on Mr. Wang's divan, tea-bowls in front of him and an opera hat beside him.

"Hein, Stella," said he, rising at her entrance, "I am very pleased to see you, but you must not tell anybody you have met me here."

Stella subsided, trembling and speechless, upon the far end of the divan and clutched her heart.

"What is the matter, Stella?" said Li, sitting down beside her.

"Nothing, I—I'm just breathless, that's all. There's nothing the matter. I got the wind up waiting in the dark and seeing things move in the shadows."

"But what brings you here at this time of the evening?"

Stella told him, and of her own miscalculation of the swiftly falling dusk.

"Hein," said Li, "your aunt knows how the dusk falls here, even if you don't. They will send you to Hell some day to fetch their cigarettes. You must never come this way after dark, my child. I can protect you by daylight, but nothing and nobody can protect you in these alleys after dark. Come, we will give you tea, and then we must see about getting you home. That is not as simple as it looks, for I dare not be seen out with you, and Mr. Wang is lame, and would be no safer than yourself in the dark, and there is not another soul in the house."

"I thought the house was empty," said Stella. "It was just a forlorn hope that I knocked at all."

"You were meant to think it was empty, my child. But how did you come to knock as you did?"

Stella told him of the man who came out of the shadows, and he appeared perturbed.

"I am ever so sorry if I have made difficulties for you," said Stella. " Let me make a bolt for it and take my chance."

"No, that is not to be thought of. Listen, Stella, I will trust you with a secret ; if you betray it, you will die in a few hours, and you will die by my hand. Now come with me."

He rose, and stepped in front of the elaborate cabinet that held the precious tea, and pulled at a knob; but instead of some small portion of it opening, the whole of it swung back bodily and revealed a flight of steep steps that led dizzily downward. Li flung the light of a powerful electric torch down them, and turned and held out his hand to Stella.

After a second's hesitation she placed hers in it, and felt again the same curious electric thrill she had felt when she had taken his arm as she stumbled over the railway ties at the dock-side in far-away Tilbury; only it was much more powerful now, for there was no thick tweed to insulate it, and her small white hand touched the living yellow flesh of this man of an alien race. Involuntarily she raised her eyes to his, but they were narrow, inscrutable slits that told her nothing.

With his help she scrambled down the precarious ladder-like stair, and found herself in a passage cut in the living rock of the cliff. Li let go her hand.

"Go ahead," he said, "and I will throw the light in front of you so that you can see where you are going."

It was the logical thing to do when there was only one torch between two people, but somehow it terrified her to have him following silently behind her like that, cat-footed in his patent leather evening shoes. The clicking of her own heels on the stone sounded so loud in comparison that she too walked on her toes, and they stole silently along in the circle of light that advanced before them into the ever-receding darkness.

Li never spoke.

To Stella it seemed that they had been walking for miles and had taken hours about it and descended down the steepest of irregular stairs to the bowels of the earth, when at last they came to a stoutly constructed door. Li put her aside, inserted a key in the lock, and it swung open. He held it for her and she stepped onto the rich thick carpet of an office furnished in modern European style with roll top desk and filing cabinets. Stella needed no telling where she was. This was the chairman's office of the Inland and Overseas Commercial Bank of China, and once the door by which they had entered was shut, it was an invisible part of the handsome panelling.

Li crossed the room and switched on the light. "Sit down, Yan Tai," he said, motioning her to the chair for interviewers beside the roll-top desk. He did not sit down himself, however, but went and stood with his back to the mantelpiece leaning his shoulders against it in their admirably cut dinner-jacket, and stared silently at the carpet. Stella, staring as steadily at him as he was staring at the carpet, thought how incongruous his high-cheekboned, slit-eyed, yellow face appeared against its background of dress clothes and office furniture.

He looked up at length.

Stella," he said abruptly, "you must keep the secret; it will cost me—everything if you betray it by so much as a hint. It will cost Wang his life, too. The man who knocked for you will be dead by morning

"Oh no Wu Lu he only did me a kindness!" cried Stella in great distress.

"He knows too much, Stella, and if I did my duty by those who trust me, you would be dead too. But I am not going to kill you; but if you betray me, I shall kill myself."

Stella, hearing him talk thus matter-of-factly of such quantities of killings, could hardly take him seriously. And yet she saw by his very matter-of-factness that he meant what he said.

She made one more desperate plea.

"Wu Lu, please don't kill the poor man who knocked for me. I shall feel simply awful about it if you do."

"I am sorry, Yan Tai, but it has got to be done. He knows too much."

"I shall never forgive you."

He raised his narrow eyes and looked at her; then he lowered them again without speaking.

"If there is anything that can impress caution on a woman, it is the knowledge that a man has died on account of her. I am sorry, Stella, but I owe that much to those who trust me. If you break with me on that account, so be it."

Stella knew that it was useless to argue with him, and sat in a huddled heap in the leather arm-chair beside the desk.

A movement close to her caused her to raise a startled head.

"Excuse me," said Li, and unlocked his desk. From one of the large lower drawers he took out a deed-box, unlocked it, and revealed, thus carefully guarded, a common blue cotton outfit such as coolies wear. Removing his coat and rolling up his trousers to the knee, he proceeded to put this on over his European clothes.

"I am going to see you safely home," he said.

"I am awfully sorry to give you such a lot of trouble," said Stella miserably.

"It doesn't matter; only don't do it again."

When he had finished, he stood up, to all outward appearance a low class Chinese. In that kit he seemed more alien and remote than ever, and Stella marvelled that she could ever have thought of him as a friend. She also thought, his kit topped off by a battered black slouch hat of the cheapest European manufacture, how extraordinarily ugly he was. The characteristic coolie smell of the clothes smote her nostrils, and she shrank from him still further.

"I must apologise for the smell," he said, "but a clean man in this kit would rouse suspicion." And she knew that her thoughts had been read with his usual uncanny accuracy.

He paused for a moment, gazing thoughtfully at his desk; then he opened one of the small inner drawers.

"I am going to give you this, Yan Tai," he said. "Never let yourself fall alive into the hands of your enemies in China," and he handed her a tiny revolver with a handle of mother of pearl "Don't shrink from it child," as she drew hastily back from the hand that proffered the weapon it is a merciful thing If that man who saw you has not died before he could talk, you may be very glad of it."

He picked up the bag that lay in her lap, opened the catch, and dropped the little gun inside it.

"Come along. The longer you are missing, the more attention you will attract. Tell your family you got on the wrong tram and missed your way."

She followed him down through the dark and silent premises of the bank, waited while he switched off the burglar alarms, and then stood silently at his heels while he peered out through a crack in the door held just ajar to watch for the coming of a tram.

"When the tram comes run along in the shadow for a few yards and then cross the road and wait under the lamp. If any one molests you I will come out and give him a crack on the head with this," and she saw that from his wrist a life-preserver hung by its thong. "I will jump on the tram as it starts and travel back with you, only for God's sake don't take any notice of me. Get off at the town hall, and you are within a few yards of your house. I will follow you back and see you safely indoors and then Yan Tai every thing is as if it had never happened You must never speak of it again and neither will I or Wang Tsang."

"I shall never go near Mr. Wang again, I've had enough," said Stella.

"You must, Stella, it is most urgent that you should. You must act just as if nothing had happened. You mustn't show by the quiver of an eyelid that you have even been frightened. Do this for me, my child, even if you never speak to me again, for I have saved you from a very terrible death to-night, and at no small risk to myself, either."

"Very well," said Stella miserably, " but I feel as if I never wanted to set eyes on a Chinaman any more."

"Two Chinamen have been good friends to you to-night, Yan Tai. Here comes your tram. Run out quickly. I am sorry you are angry with me, my star."

Without a backward glance or word of thanks, Stella darted across the road diagonally as bid. She boarded the tram, being liberally stared at by its rough cargo of all the colours in creation, for this was a water-front tram that came up from the lowest docks. She glanced round anxiously for her escort, but there was no sign of him. Then, as the tram gathered speed, she heard the conductor curse, and saw a coolie swing himself onto the swiftly moving vehicle. She never looked round, but stared fixedly in front of her till the town hail was reached, and then she got off without a backward glance and walked quickly up the tree-bordered road to Esperanza House. Whether she were followed, and by whom, she never knew, for she never looked round to see.

Esperanza House she found in an uproar, her aunt in hysterics, and her uncle swearing at her like a trooper. He, at any rate, was alive to the danger of sending a young girl alone into the Chinese quarter in the dusk, and had some conscience in the matter.

CHAPTER VII

IT was a long time before Stella got to sleep that night; her experience in the Chinese quarter had been a considerable shock to her; far more of a shock than appeared to be necessary on the face of it. After all, nothing had been done to her, or even threatened, as she had stood in the dusk on the step of Mr. Wang's house. True, Mr. Li had threatened her with dire consequences, but in a matter-of-fact manner that took all the sting out of it; and looked at impartially, the discovery of the secret of the underground passage that connected the magnificent buildings of the Inland and Overseas Commercial Bank with the old curio-dealer's ramshackle shop was a great adventure, and the surreptitious escape by that furtive route a great lark. She knew that that was the light in which the stolid Rosemary would have viewed it. Then why could she not? True, Mr. Li had threatened to kill her; but then, he had taken it back and said he wasn't going to kill her, but would kill himself instead— all very calm and unsensational, so that it seemed just a manner of speaking. The only thing that was really nasty was the threat that the man who had done her a kindness must die for doing it. That really did upset her. There was some thing so dreadful and cruel about it. Stella thought of his family in their grief and destitution, and reduced herself to tears.

But although she might genuinely feel for the fate of the unknown coolie and his family, it did not account for the profound disturbance she felt. She could not understand it. She tried to analyse it, and the nearest she could come to an answer was that it was perfectly rotten of Li Wu Lu to kill that coolie.

She determined that she would use the opportunity afforded by her promise to go down to Wang's next day to put in an impassioned plea for the unfortunate victim of his own kindness, for she could hardly believe that they could have arranged his murder so quickly.

Next morning, left to her own devices, she would gladly have stopped in bed, for what with a sleepless night on top of a fright, she felt a wreck. However, to have admitted to any indisposition would have been to admit the existence of unpleasantness, and once admissions began there was no knowing where they might end if her aunt set to work to cross-examine and observe her. Moreover, there was her promise to Li that she would act exactly as if nothing had happened, and she felt that she owed him at least the fulfilment of that promise after all the trouble he had gone to on her behalf the previous evening. He had obviously cut a party of some sort, creased his dress trousers, and boarded a moving tram at the risk of his neck. She certainly owed him something, even if she discounted his melodramatics about all the murders and suicides and general bloodshed and devastation, and like all people who have never met violence face to face, she found it very easy to do that.

So Stella set off for Chinatown next morning, a little heavy-eyed, it is true, but otherwise self-possessed.

But as soon as she passed through the clumsy mud arch that always seemed in some queer way to be sinister, she felt her tension return. There was a queer feel about the quarter, too, it was unusually quiet, and the streets were unusually empty. She fancied that people stared at her with more curiosity than was normal. She hurried along, becoming more and more nervous as she advanced into that warren of mean alleys, clutching her bag hard against her beating heart, till the pressure of an unfamiliar shape reminded her that it held the little revolver Li had given her, and the memory brought a sense of relief. For it seemed to her that if he intended any evil against her, he would not have given her a revolver, and she realised with a start that the thing which was upsetting her was really her fear of Li. What she feared, or why she feared, or what had started her fearing her friend, she did not know.

Finally she arrived breathless on the threshold of Mr.

Wang's shop. It stood open as usual, but the vegetable dealer's across the way was closed, and Stella remembered with a shock Mr. Li's threat that the man who had knocked for her must die because he knew too much, and it was from one of those mean shops, little better than stalls, on the opposite side of the road that the unlucky Samaritan had come.

Stella entered the cool darkness of the curio shop, and Mr. Wang, as neat and prim as ever, rose from his low seat beside his floor desk to bow to her.

Stella wasted no time on Oriental politeness.

"What has happened to the man across the way?" she demanded.

"I do not know," said Wang, impassive as a Sphinx. Stella looked at him, and he looked at Stella, and she knew that it was hopeless; she might just as well have knocked on the Pyramids with her bare knuckles for all the response she would be able to elicit.

So with a sigh she followed him into the long low building out at the back where the surplus stock was stored, and set to work to clean and sort some newly arrived purchases, for Mr. Wang believed, and rightly, that it was only possible to learn to understand curios by constantly handling them. Like all Chinese houses, Mr. Wang's emporium presented blank walls to the world, its windows looking onto an inner courtyard, an exclusive but stuffy custom; Stella, glancing out of the windows as she worked, saw to her surprise that Wang's daughter-in-law was busily engaged in washing a European dress shirt; looking more closely, she saw that the daughter-in-law was having a great job getting blood stains out of the cuffs.

Stella went straight back into the shop.

"I want to speak to you," she said to Mr. Wang. He rose obediently and conducted her into his little sanctum.

"I have just seen your daughter-in-law washing the bloodstains out of the shirt that Mr. Li was wearing last night. What does it mean?"

Wang rubbed his chin thoughtfully.

"It is no good telling me again that you do not know," said

78

Stella tartly.

"I know some things, but I do not know all, honourable virgin. But I know enough to know that it is better not to know too much."

"Will you tell me what you know?"

"No, honourable virgin, I will tell you nothing."

"I am going home."

"If the honourable virgin would condescend to wait a little, one might come who could tell her something."

Stella returned to her task in the out-house with a beating heart, and inside five minutes Li walked in, dressed in the shantung lounge suit that was the usual business wear of Europeans.

"Hein, Stella ?" said he, "what is it you want to know?"

Given a dose of her own Occidental downrightness, Stella was just as taken aback as an Oriental would have been.

"I want to know what has happened to that poor man who helped me last night."

"He is dead, and a lot more will be dead, too, before long."

"Who killed him?"

"He died."

"Were you present when he died?

"I was."

"What did he die of?"

"Why go into these horrors, Stella? You will not like them."

"Did you torture him?"

Li hesitated for a split second, and then said: "No."

"Then how did you come to get blood on the cuffs of your dress shirt?"

Li's brows drew together in a frown.

"You want to know too much, little star. You have seen me close one mouth. If you are not careful you may see me close another. I have more at stake than is worth the life of one girl, however pretty."

Stella felt a pang of fear go through her, and shrank back involuntarily.

"Yes, it is good for you to be frightened, spoilt child of the

West."

"I am not frightened," said Stella, lifting her head defiantly, "I—I am sort of horrified."

That was indeed the truth, and Li, looking closely at her, noted her white, drawn face and heavy eyes. His face lost its ferocity.

"I am sorry, little star, it has been an awkward business for everybody. What is it you are horrified at? Just Chinese life in general? It is no use being horrified at that. I am Chinese, and you must take me as you find me."

"Wu Lu, why did that man have to die for being kind to me?"

"He did not die for being kind to you, Yan Tai, he died for being a fool."

"But the whole street knew I had got into the house. They were all poking their heads out to see what was happening."

"Yes, but the whole street did not know how you got in. Listen, Stella, and I will try and make it clear. I am sorry I told you anything. You have taken it differently from what I expected. You are more unlike our girls than I had realised. It was a mistake to try and frighten you. I will deal with you as if you were a man. I am going to trust you, Stella, and that is a thing I have never done with any woman before, or ever heard of being done; if you are indiscreet, let alone treacherous, it will cost me my life. Now listen, and try and understand. Try and see things from the point of view of people who are hanging onto life very precariously. I am deeply involved with the Tongs—you know what they are?

Stella nodded.

"That man across the road must have watched, and observed, and spied upon this house, for he had learnt the secret knocks that are given by members of my Tong to gain admission. No common, ignorant vegetable-seller would have troubled to do that, therefore some one must have put him on to do it.

"As you rightly guessed, I—questioned—that man to find out who he was. And I found what I expected. I learnt that he was not a common vegetable-seller at all, but an educated man in the employ of your secret police. Stella, could I let him go back to your police headquarters, and tell his chief that you had come down to this house to meet me—for that was what it looked like—and have the police chief, who is a friend of your uncle's, tell him that you had been down here, and had met me, and not left by the door, but reappeared some time later on a dockside tram? And then have them try to ferret out your relationship with me And enquire among the stewards on board the liner, and possibly hear the purser's version of it? What do you suppose they would believe your relationship with me was? Would any one believe the truth? Who was I to sacrifice, you or the spy? You, being a Christian, might have scruples, but I, being Chinese, had none. The spy is dead, and you are safe. Hein, Stella, would you make that spy alive again if you could? Answer me that, will you?"

"No, I—expect I wouldn't, though I suppose I ought to. It seems so awfully cruel that he did me a disinterested kindness and had to suffer so for it."

"Did you think that was a disinterested kindness, Stella? Not a bit of it. It was an opportunity for blackmail. He must have known I was in the house, though how he knew, God only knows. I had thought that house was safe if any thing was. No, Stella, no Chinese ever does a disinterested kindness, don't you believe it."

"Then—why did you let me have that cabin—and—and put me in touch with Mr. Wang?"

Li's jaw dropped in so marked a manner that Stella was nearly as taken aback as he was. He did not reply, but walked over to the window and stood looking out into the cluttered courtyard where his own shirt now hung stainless on the line. He stood thus for quite a while without speaking, and then he came walking back again with an impassive face and stood in front of Stella.

"I am going to tell you the truth," he said, as if it were something quite exceptional. "That is a trick I learnt in England, and it is very disconcerting to the Asiatic. We will see how it suits you.

"As I told you on board ship, I am an Oriental with an Occidental education. I was sent to England at the age of twelve, and did not return to China until I was twenty-four, my father coming over each year to visit our London branch and spend the summer vacation with me. That was a mistake. When I got back to China, I could not settle down; Chinese life was too narrow for me. Before I left for England, I had been married to the daughter of a friend of our family; when I came back, she was handed over to me. She was a well-brought-up young woman with the brain of a rabbit; they had never even troubled to teach her to read. I had picked up other ideas on the subject of marriage in England, and she was no use to me. I did my duty by her, which was all that was required of me, and she died with her first child.

"My grandfather, who is old-fashioned, wanted to find me another wife, but I said no; it had been a sickening business, and I would have no more of it. I had one or two fairly thorough disillusionments, and after that I accepted life as it had been made for me,"

"I suppose that means you settled down with your eight concubines," interrupted Stella.

"Hein? You don't like my concubines, do you, Stella? No, it meant nothing of the sort, but we won't go into that; revelations of Chinese life don't seem to agree with you. And I haven't got eight concubines now, I have only got seven."

"Did one run away while you were in Europe?"

"No, two ran away, and I have replaced one."

He looked at Stella's crestfallen face, and began to laugh. "Hein, you are a baby, Stella! You don't understand my concubines a bit, do you?"

"They are the parlour-maids?"

"No, they are the safety-valves. And the new one is fire insurance. Don't be silly, Stella, you are a little goose. Anyway, concubines have their uses. They are mildly decorative if nothing more. But they are not companions; one cannot make friends of them. Now what I liked about you was that one could make a friend of you.

"But I knew that if I made a friend of you openly there would be a terrible outcry; the Chinese would be angry with me, and the English would be angry with you. Consequently such friendship as I was able to enjoy with you had to be sub rosa—and still has to be—Stella, for that matter. I was very glad to be able to oblige you over the cabin, and I am very glad to have been instrumental in putting you on to a job with Mr. Wang, which will, I hope, in due time make you independent of your very unattractive relations. And if you like, we will have tea together sometimes, like we did on board ship, but that is the beginning and end of it. Would you like that?"

"I should like it very much," said Stella, "for I am deadly lonely."

"So am I, Stella," said Li, with a sudden flash of his dark eyes, "but it is no use thinking of anything else."

He looked at his watch.

"Hein, I must get back; there will be some very angry men at the bank."

Mr. Wang ambling in presently to see how the work was getting on, looked at Stella sharply out of his narrow eyes, and saw her all flushed and happy where previously she had been pale and miserable, and his narrow eyes grew still narrower.

That day, on her way home to lunch, Stella entered a silk shop, and there purchased several lengths of the slightly flawed silk that is sold so cheaply in such places. At another shop she bought one of the slightly imperfect straw hats that are cast out when the consignments of hand-woven hoods come in from the villages for the European market, thus coming by a fine imitation Bangkok, indistinguishable from a genuine one save by an expert, for a few pence. Then she and the amah spent a very pleasant afternoon engaged in needlework.

The result was startling. Whereas the fussy elaboration and obvious colourings of Rosemary's cast-offs had completely destroyed whatever claims Stella might have to good looks, the simple grace of her own designs and the exquisite colourings of the native silks revealed her unusual dark charms.

It is true that Rosemary's young men had stared at her

more in bewilderment than admiration, and shown a strong disinclination to being seen out in her company, and Rosemary had giggled that her frocks looked like nightgowns, but Mr. Hope had expressed the opinion that she looked a damn sight better in them than he had ever seen her look before, and Mr. Mathers, the connoisseur of Chinese curios, had said to her as he bowed over her hand with old-fashioned courtesy:

"Miss Stella, do you know that you are going to develop into a uniquely beautiful woman?

Stella was very thrilled, and wondered what effect her new frocks would have on Li when he should turn up for the promised tea-party.

Old Wang chuckled softly when he saw her for the first time in her new-style dresses, and produced with great ceremony a necklet of tawny topaz, almost the colour of old port, expressing the pious hope that it might prove auspicious to the wearer as he laid it tenderly in her hands.

And that very afternoon Li did turn up for the promised tea-party. When he saw Stella, innocently preening in her new frock, his eyes glittered.

"Ha, Stella, that suits you," he said. "I should like to see you wearing rubies with that."

"I couldn't possibly take rubies from you, Wu Lu," she said.

"No, I know you couldn't, but will you please me by wearing them if I send for them?"

"Oh, yes, I'll wear them to please you if you like."

He disappeared back into the shop, for their tea-table was laid in a place cleared in the seclusion of the big go-down, safe from the intrusion of chance customers. In a little while he was back, with a small steel box of European manufacture in his hand. He opened it with an intricate key, and took out first one tray and then another. From among their contents he selected a pendant made of a single enormous ruby of true pigeon's blood red and almost a pigeon's egg in size. He searched further, and selected a ring, also made of a unique single stone; then from the depths of the box he picked out a bracelet made in the form of a golden snake with a ruby head, that coiled up into a tight spiral as it lay in its case. These he held out towards her in the palm of his hand.

"Put these on, please," he said.

She picked them up one by one from his palm and did as she was bid. Then they performed the tea-ritual, Stella admiring as she did so the flash of the jewels on wrist and finger. Mr. Li seemed completely denuded of small talk, and did nothing but sit and gaze at the flashing splendour of his gems as they caught the light with Stella's movements.

At the conclusion of the ceremonial meal he packed them back again into their case.

"Hein," he said, looking at Stella with expressionless eyes. "The glory is departed," and stalked off without any other form of farewell. Stella felt vaguely disappointed. It had not been an altogether satisfactory tea-party, but she did not know quite what was wrong with it.

Next time Li turned up to tea, he did not suggest she should wear the jewels again, and she was thankful; somehow, she had not enjoyed wearing those jewels. It put her too much in mind of the concubines.

Those tea-parties were fairly frequent. Never less than two, sometimes as many as four a week. Presently Stella heard it remarked at her uncle's dinner-table that Mr. Li, who had hitherto always been most punctual and business-like, had recently taken to cutting appointments in a truly Oriental fashion and giggled inwardly. But the next remark stopped her giggle abruptly.

"I expect he's got a new concubine," said her uncle.

CHAPTER VIII

STELLA was given to think furiously by what she had heard at the dinner-table. She had thought that business had been slack with Mr. Li, and that he had been dropping in to kill time; but apparently business was far from slack, but he could not be got to attend to it. She was not very experienced in human nature, and especially male human nature on the sunny side of senility, but she saw quite clearly that Li was acting with her exactly as if he had got a new concubine, and asked herself what it meant?

She knew that the Chinese banker liked being with her, but she had no means of knowing how much he liked her, for he had always been very uncommunicative on that point. There had never been one word or look of sentimentality; in fact he treated her, and she treated him, just as if he were one of her father's old friends, long since dried almost to powder by the air of the Museum reading-room. There had never been anything, or any hint of anything, to which the strictest chaperon could take exception. Mr. Li was discretion and sedateness itself, save for that brief occasion when he had lost his temper on board ship, and then his wrath had not been directed at her.

She asked herself frankly what she felt about him, and admitted equally frankly that she found him very attractive, and that life would be very dull without the tea-parties. She knew perfectly well that she had taken her frocks in hand in anticipation of those tea-parties, and that Mr. Wang had spotted as much when he had added the topaz necklet to her costume, She wondered whether Mr. Li had noticed anything, or whether Wang had dropped a hint. But that she had no means of knowing, for the Chinese are inscrutable to Western eyes till after very long acquaintance.

"Well," thought Stella to herself, "I think Wu Lu is being naughty, but I don't think he intends any harm. And anyway, it is not my responsibility if he keeps all these business men waiting, or even forgets about them altogether. Let them fight it out between them."

So the tea-parties went on. Li was a trifle moody at times. Sometimes he would lay aside his dignity and behave like a schoolboy, and sometimes he would withdraw into himself abruptly, and become very formal or even sullen, and clear out back to the bank with the scantiest of excuses and the curtest of farewells.

Then one day the tea-parties ceased abruptly, and no explanation offered. As the gap lengthened, Stella became more and more desolate, and found herself listening for every step, till at last she could bear it no more, and put aside her pride and asked Mr. Wang if he knew what had become of Li.

"He has gone to the funeral of his grandfather," said Mr. Wang.

"Why ever didn't he tell me?"

"He said you were to be told if you asked."

Stella gathered her pride together sufficiently not to ask when he was expected back, and Mr. Wang did not vouchsafe any information on that point. Presumably he had been told to say nothing unless asked, and Stella was not going to show her hand any further by asking. Li could turn up again when he felt like it. If he were angling to find out what she felt about him, he just wasn't going to know, any more than she knew what he really felt about her.

The ensuing weeks were very trying ones. Mrs. Hope sensed unconsciously that Stella was under the weather and began to bully her, at first with just the passing irritability of a nervy woman, and then with the steady nagging persistence of one who enjoys persecuting. Stella, missing Li increasingly as the weeks lengthened out and she heard nothing from him, and not knowing how long a Chinese funeral might reasonably be expected to take, or whether he had got a yet newer concubine and had begun to cut his appointments with her in their turn, was an easy victim for a domestic torturer, and one of those horrible conditions built up that occur when a woman whom life has not satisfied gets a young girl into her power. Life at Esperanza House was well-nigh intolerable, and the hours at Mr. Wang's shop were the only things that prevented Stella from going completely to pieces under the treatment she was receiving.

Then, when she had almost given up hope of ever renewing her friendship with Li, he walked into the go-down as she worked and greeted her with his usual queer nasal grunt:

"Hein, Stella, how are you?"

She told him her troubles, and ended up in tears.

"Hein," said Li noncommittally, offering no sympathy. "I must get back to the bank, there are people waiting for me," and turned on his heel and left her.

But for some time after that she heard him talking to Mr. Wang in the sanctum behind the shop, and sometimes his voice was raised very imperiously.

Stella, who concluded that she had finished off what was left of the friendship by her untimely tears, shed some more and became more dispirited than ever.

Presently old Wang drifted in to talk to her as she worked, as his custom was; but to-day he did not talk of Chinese art, but of personalities, a thing he had never done before. No names were mentioned, and he was discretion itself, but nevertheless, he was talking, and his words were to the point.

"A great loss has been sustained," he said. Stella expressed regret.

"One who has been more than a father."

Stella invoked the blessing of heaven upon the bereaved.

"A young man needs a steadying influence," said Wang, gazing fixedly at a very sinister-looking image of a deity dedicated to war and pestilence.

Stella wondered at what age a man was considered mature in this land of ancestor worship. She was immensely tickled, in spite of her melancholy, by the idea of the influential banker needing a guiding hand.

Wang shook his head mournfully, and appeared absorbed in gloomy speculation, which considering the object he was gazing at, was very understandable.

"The outlook gives rise to anxiety," he said. "The restraining hand being removed—" and with one last, long lingering look at the depressing countenance of the god of war and pestilence, he took himself off.

Stella knew that a hint had been given her, but owing to Mr. Wang's extreme discretion, she did not know quite what it was meant to convey. Was Li neglecting his business, and was she being asked not to encourage too many tea-parties? Or was she being warned that now that his grandfather was no longer there to keep him in order, he might kick over the traces? Stella, judging Li to be somewhere in the neighbourhood of forty and marvellously lucky to have had a grandfather so long, thought the latter interpretation unlikely, especially in view of his complete lack of sympathy for her in her troubles, which she really thought was rather beastly of him. As for his slacking at the office, that was absolutely no business of hers; in the mood she was in, she was fed to the teeth with life and almost at the end of her tether; she didn't care if he set the bank on fire in his youthful irresponsibility, she would let things take their course whatever it might be. Li Wu Lu was quite well able to take care of himself, and needed no supervision from her, or from Mr. Wang either, for that matter.

The following morning, sitting in the lounge waiting for the belated breakfast to start, Stella Was passing the time away by turning over the pages of a very fine illustrated book on Chinese art that Mr. Mathers had lent her aunt under the delusion that she was interested in such things, When she came upon a reproduction of an early Chinese painting of Kwan Yin, the goddess of mercy, 'in her Aphrodite aspect as Yan Tai, the Supremely Desirable One; from the collection of Mr. Li Wu Lu.' Stella felt her spirits rise perceptibly.

And she needed them. For a dance was being given at Esperanza House that evening, and she was expected to make herself useful in preparing for it; Mrs. Hope had worn herself to a frazzle with dieting, and was a poor organiser anyway, but what she lacked in directing power she made up for in driving-force. Stella never was off her feet, and had no proper meal, from the time she got up from the breakfast table till the guests began to arrive.

Consequently she was absolutely worn out; and so, for the matter of that, was her aunt. But whereas Mrs. Hope retired to the bathroom for a few minutes, to reappear miraculously rejuvenated, Stella, not having access to what the medicine-cupboard contained, had to endure as best she could.

The guests duly arrived, but not the band; and when the spate of arrivals began to slacken off, Mrs. Hope shot out into the outer hall where Stella was shepherding the servants, and hissed in her ear:

"Did you remember to order the band?"

"Good Lord, no, you never asked me to!" exclaimed Stella.

Mrs. Hope hit her a resounding smack on the cheek regardless of the watching eyes of the servants of the house and the assorted chauffeurs of the guests.

Stella, knocked off her balance by the force of the blow, went cannoning backwards into some one's arms, who, luckily for her, held her up. Looking half-dazed over her shoulder to see who or what she had hit, Stella saw looking down the expressionless yellow face of Mr. Li. He bowed formally, set her on her feet, and went on into the ballroom without speaking. Mrs. Hope had already rushed off to the study to try and get on the phone to the band, and was in any case too frantic to have known or cared who had witnessed her outburst.

Stella, what with the blow given her in front of the servants and the snub direct she had received from Mr. Li, was no longer tearful, but in the state of cold rage that some temperaments are liable to when pushed too far.

Mrs. Hope rushed back from the study.

"I can't get the band! Stella, go and put on the gramo-phone."

"I won't!" said Stella, her eyes blazing.

"You'll find yourself in the gutter if you don't," shouted

90

Mrs. Hope, and rushed off again in the direction of the ball-room.

Stella, bitterly swallowing her wrath, went off to do as she was bid. Making her way across the wide expanse of the dancing floor amid the waiting couples, she saw Mr. Li bowing over the hand of her aunt, both of them smiling most genially as if nothing had ever happened.

Arrived at the gramophone behind its screen of palms, she wound up the spring, put on a record, and the dance began. Watching the crowd through the screen of leaves, Stella put on record after record, and the evening wore itself away. Various special items were planned to enliven the proceedings, had they stood in any need of enlivening after the wine got in its work; there was a Paul Jones, a cotillion, and a leap-year waltz; finally, with Mr. Hope manipulating rather erratically a spot-light from the gallery, there was a dance wherein all the lights went out, and whatever lady was illuminated by the spot-light when the music stopped, was to have a present. Stella, the gramophone attending to itself, stood watching this eerie performance.

Suddenly she was startled by a light touch on her wrist, and then a hand closed over hers. She turned, indignant. It was too dark to see faces, and all she could make out was the loom of a white shirt-front; but there came to her nostrils the faint sweet smell of the sandalwood chests in which wealthy Chinese kept their clothes. Stella's hand quivered for a moment, and then lay still.

For a while neither moved; than at length Li said in a low voice:

"You have no need to stay here any longer than you want to, Stella, I am my own master now. Come to Wang's early to-morrow morning, and we will talk things over."

She felt her hand released. The music stopped. Squeals of excitement saluted the staggers of the spot-light, and finally a giggling maiden and her swain went up to Mr. Hope to receive a box of chocolates. As soon as they were disposed of, she saw Li making his adieux to his hostess.

Round about three o'clock the dance petered out. Stella,

who had done no inconsiderable amount of manual labour in winding the gramophone, made a scratch meal off the remains of the buffet, and lay down exhausted on her bed, removing no more than her dress. Mr. Li had said: Be at Wang's early, and she meant to snatch a short sleep and get there and back before the rest of the family were out of their belated beds. So she set her alarm clock and lay down in her clothes. Duly aroused by the clock, she made her breakfast of what was left of the ball supper, which looked horribly like garbage as it lay in disorder among dirty plates, faded flowers and battered favours on the stained tablecloth, Feeling in need of a restorative of some sort, Stella drank some flat champagne; it was an effectual pick-me-up, but not conducive to clear thinking.

Then she set out by tram for the terminus beside the mud gate that gave access to the native city. She was well known here by now, had made many friends, and could come and go in complete security, exchanging greetings all down the street. But to-day her Chinese friends found her absent minded, returning their politenesses perfunctorily, or failing to notice them altogether. For Stella was trying to do a little thinking; the night before she had been too utterly exhausted to string two ideas together, and now the champagne she had indiscreetly taken in the hope of pulling herself together was not proving at all helpful, presenting everything in a lurid light.

She wished to heaven she hadn't taken it, for the one thing she wanted above all others was to have her wits about her. Some sort of a decision would have to be taken upon the proposition Mr. Li intended to put before her, and it might have far-reaching repercussions. She was particularly anxious not to drop such another brick with him as she had dropped when she dissolved into tears in his presence; she had always heard that men hated that sort of thing, and she had had conclusive proof that they did. Mr. Li, who could be very sympathetic when he chose, had not been at all responsive on that occasion.

But then she had a very clear recollection of those few moments when he had stood silently in the dark with her hand in his. What did that mean? In the case of one of Rosemary's young men it would have meant absolutely nothing, a certain amount of necking being the small change of social intercourse in the Hopes' set. But in the case of the formal and reserved Li Wu Lu, what might it be taken to mean? It was one thing for a boy of her own set to hold her hand at a dance, but quite another for a man in Li's position, and of Li's restrained, self-disciplined temperament, to break through the cast-iron racial taboo and touch her thus. At the time she had been so upset and over-wrought that she had not realised the significance of the hand that had sought hers, but had clung to her friend's hand like a frightened child; but now, in the cold light of morning, going to keep her appointment with him, she began to do some pretty hard thinking, and she prayed that the champagne, which she mistrusted, would keep quiet and let her think clearly and act wisely.

She did not deny to herself, had never denied, that she was in love with Li; and she had suspected all along that he was very attracted towards her; but she also knew, not by inference but by plain statement, that he had no intention of compromising himself with her. She knew, however, from the hint Mr. Wang had given her, and from Li's own words, that the death of his grandfather, the head of his house, had made an enormous difference to both his position and his attitude.

Did it mean that now he was free from over-riding authority, Li would ask her to marry him, and if so what would she do about it? Stella was under no delusions with regard to mixed marriages; she knew that the pressure that is brought to bear upon them is practically intolerable, and however good the man himself might be, there were very few who could stand the abnormal strain, and what could have been a happy marriage under normal conditions, cracked up under the abnormal ones. It took two very exceptional people to make a success of a mixed marriage.

Of course Li might merely have some sort of business proposition to put before her—financing her in a curio shop, most likely; he had hinted at something of the sort more than once, as if sounding her. He might be as disinclined as ever to face the social odium that a mixed marriage would involve for him just as much as for her. She must keep herself well in hand, and not jump to the conclusion that Li was bent on romance, because the Chinese are a very unromantic race in actual practice, whatever they may be in theory.

But supposing he did ask her to marry him, what would be her answer? Stella knew without any hesitation what it would have been if he had belonged to her own race—but would she face the difficulties of a mixed marriage?

"I shall certainly never marry any one else," said Stella to herself. "He's finished that for me, anyway. It would be no use to marry any one else, feeling as I do about him. Life with the family is intolerable; I can't possibly be worse off with him than I am now. I can't go on, I shall simply crack up. And I think he really is an awfully fine man; everything I have seen of him points that way; and everyone seems to think so, even those who dislike the Chinese in the ordinary way. Every one says he's straight, and every one says he's awfully clever. Yes, if he asks me to marry him, I'll do it. But all the same I must be careful not to show the slightest sign that I've ever thought of that, or I shall look an awful fool if he simply means to put me on to a job. I wish to goodness I hadn't drunk that champagne!"

What with her hurried walk and her beating heart, she arrived at the curio shop so breathless she was speechless. Mr. Wang seated beside his low desk, as if he had spent the night there unmoving, looked at her with totally expressionless, uninterested eyes.

"The honourable virgin is expected," he said. "Will she go up to the Coffin Room?

This invitation was not quite so sinister as it sounded., Mr. Wang, like most well-to-do Chinese, had provided himself with a coffin that was the choicest thing he possessed. It really was a magnificent work of art, and to be asked to inspect it was the greatest honour that could be done to a visitor. It occupied a prominent position in what would have been the drawing-room of a European house, and the importance he attached to the interview which was about to take place was indicated by the fact that it was to be staged in the ceremonial apartment occupied by the coffin, and not in the corner of the go-down, where the tea-parties had always taken place.

Stella, her heart beating wildly, climbed up the rickety bamboo staircase, little more than a ladder, that led to the upper floor of the ramshackle house, thinking, as she always did, how it would burn if it ever caught fire; in fact, the whole quarter was one gigantic fire-lighter. Arrived at the top, she pushed open the heavy, elaborately decorated door of the Coffin Room, and entered, hardly able to breathe in her agitation. The first thing that confronted her was the coffin, acting as an efficient draught-screen in front of the door. For a moment she thought the room was empty, and then she caught sign of Mr. Li's back as he leant with his elbows on the window-sill, gazing out. He was dressed in a white linen suit, which is more formal wear than the usual office shantung, and that, together with the fact that he was awaiting her in the Coffin Room, gave Stella a yet further realisation of the importance he attached to the interview.

The creak of a board under her foot made him turn round.

"Hein, Stella? Good morning. Have you got over the dance?"

"No, I haven't. It will be a long time before I get over that dance. It was the ghastliest entertainment I have ever been at"

"Yes, I agree with you. Those entertainments—there is nothing to do but get drunk at them. If one remains sober, one is miserable."

Stella noticed that he was talking very chi-chi.

She stood hesitating in the middle of the floor. There was nothing to sit on save a kind of couch that ran down one side of the room, on which they would have had to perch side by side like birds on a twig, not at all a convenient attitude for the discussion of important business

Li solved the problem, temporarily, at any rate.

"Come over here, Stella," he said. "I want to show you something."

Relieved at heart, for this did not sound like a proposal, Stella joined him in the window, which jutted out from the room in a kind of oriel. To the right the harbour lay sheer beneath them; in front rose a steepish rocky bluff against which the far end of the go-down backed; below lay the Wang family's little *pleasaunce*.

"You see that garden up there? "said Li, pointing to the high wall that crowned the bluff, over which the tops of shrubs and the roof of a summer-house were just visible. "Well, there is a house in that garden which belongs to me. I bought it once when there was trouble going on down here, and made a way through from the go-down into the summer-house so that I could get out that way if need be. It has been very useful on several occasions. The boundary of the Concession runs along the top of that bill. In fact, it is actually marked by the garden wall in one place. The back of the house is Chinese, but the front is a shop in the Gordon Road. You may know it; it is next door to the place where your cousin goes for the ice-cream sodas that make her so fat."

"Yes, I know it," said Stella calmly, folding the idea of a proposal up small and sitting on it. " It is supposed to be tangled up in a lawsuit, isn't it?"

"That is what I have caused to be known in order to explain why it stands empty so long. No, there is no lawsuit. It belongs to me, though in another name. Now it is in my mind, Stella, that it would be a very good scheme to open a branch of Wang's shop there, so as to deal direct with Europeans and get the higher prices. It is a cut-rate trade he does here with the dealers. He could continue down here, and do the buying and pricing, and you could take charge up there, and do the selling. How would you like that, hein? The old house behind the shop could be made very nice, Stella, very nice indeed. It would be a home for you, and you would be independent."

"It sounds very good,' ' said Stella calmly; "but how does Mr. Wang like the idea?"

"Oh, he likes it very well indeed. But it would make no difference if he didn't. The business does not belong to him, it belongs to me. He is only the manager. You would be working for me up there; would you mind that, Stella?"

"Not in the least. Why should I mind it?"

"Hein, I don't know. Girls are queer. Well, would you like to work for me, or do you think I would work you too hard?"

"No, I don't think you will. But if you did I could always give notice."

"Could you, Stella? I wonder."

"Well, couldn't I?"

"You didn't think I would really make you work, did you—Yan Tai?"

Stella coloured faintly at the name. It was the first time she had heard him use it since she knew its meaning, and the way he spoke it gave it significance.

His eyes flashed as he saw her change colour.

"Hein, Stella, you have found out the meaning of that name?"

"I saw it was the name of a picture in your collection."

"Yes, that is right. I have the picture. She is very like you. You know all about her?"

"No."

"Well, she is the goddess that makes dreams come true. Will you come and keep shop for me in the house on the cliff—Yan Tai?"

Stella felt a hand laid on her shoulder, very gently. She turned round and faced the man beside her. His dark eyes, sparkling, were watching her closely.

"What exactly does that mean, Wu Lu?" she said steadily.

"It means this, little star, that if I married you, much as I should like to, we should both be outcast, for my people would outcast me just as much as the English would outcast you; but if you go up to the Gordon Road, and run a business in the front part of the shop in partnership with Wang Tsang, we can lead our own life in the Chinese part of the house that lies behind, and no one will ever be the wiser."

"Are you suggesting that I should become your mistress?" said Stella in an expressionless voice.

"Well, Stella, it would not help you if I married you; you would be just as much outcast as if you lived openly in sin. Whereas if no one knows we are in touch with each other, you will have no difficulties. You would like to come to me, wouldn't you, little star? I would like very much to have you."

"Will you tell me what I have done that makes you think you could make me an offer like that?"

"Well—Stella—you like me, don't you? You have never left me in any doubt as to that."

"Yes, I don't deny I like you; but what have I done that made you think I would ever be willing to become your mistress

"Well—Stella—wouldn't you be? Marriage is out of the question for both of us, you see that, don't you, dear? I will make you just as secure as if you were married to me. I thought I would settle the business on you under cover of a partnership with Wang, and also put some funds for you in European securities. I'll see you safe, little star, whatever happens to me. How do you feel about it?

"I feel as if you had thrown a bucket of slops over me."

"What do you mean, Stella? You think my love an insult?"

"I think your suggestion is."

"What has changed you? You have never been like this to me before. Don't tease me, Stella, I can't stand it."

"If I had thought that this was in your mind, do you think I would ever have had anything to do with you?

"Well, what did you think was in my mind?"

"You told me yourself. You said there could be no question of anything save friendship between us."

"You believed that?"

"I did. Wasn't it true?"

"Yes, I suppose it was. I thought I could do like Englishmen do, and have a friendship with you; but I found I couldn't."

"Then why didn't you break with me if you didn't want to get mixed up with me?"

"I tried to, Stella."

"When?"

"On board ship. I never meant to see you again. I didn't

realise how much you cared."

"How do you know I cared?"

"Well, you cried all night, didn't you?"

"How do you know I cried all night?"

"Because I sat on the edge of the bath all night, listening to you."

"Then I think you might have done something to help me."

"Good God, child, wasn't I doing all I could for you in parting with you ? Do you think I wanted to part with you? It was breaking my heart."

"Then, having parted and got it over, why did you come back?"

"Because I couldn't stand it. I had sworn a solemn oath in front of the tablets of my ancestors that I would go right away for three months and try and forget you. Every one thought I had gone away on business—politics—intrigue, God knows what; but I hadn't; I was up at the place where my family are all buried—alone—living Chinese fashion, no books, no papers, no letters even, everything put behind me."

I kept my oath, though I do not think I slept for the last fortnight. Then I came back. I said: I will see her once, and see if she still has the same glamour for me, or if I have exaggerated it; maybe I shall find her surrounded by young men, having a good time; it is a very gay household she is going to. And then I found you sitting alone in the car, and I knew how things were with you, knowing that household. And I thought: Stella cannot possibly be any worse off with me than she is with them."

"And then you set to work to stalk me?" Stella interrupted.

"No. No, Stella; no, I didn't. I swear I didn't. I thought it would be enough for me if I could just be friends with you. It wasn't the other side of you I wanted. That is commonplace enough. I can buy that for a few dollars. Any Chinese woman could give me that. It was something very different that you gave me. Then I found it wouldn't work. I am not a white man. My blood is too hot. You are too attractive, Stella."

"When did you realise that?"

"When you wore my jewels. But it had been coming on for some time. I can see that now, looking back. I think it started that night you came in all frightened, like a little bird, and I had to look after you. Stella, I would have killed the whole quarter for you, that night

"You never showed anything of this."

"No, no, of course I didn't. I am not a fool. And you didn't see anything, did you? You thought you could go on being ever so friendly to a man who was in love with you, and nothing ever come of it? I said once you were a baby, Stella; I was wrong, you are a foetus."

"But if you felt like this about me, why did you buy a new concubine?"

"Stella, need you ask? Don't be silly."

"And you now are offering me the job of ninth concubine? Or is it eighth ? I can't remember, I have lost count."

"Hein, it is easy to get a rise out of you with my concubines, you are so jealous of them. No, there are no concubines now, Stella. I have disposed of them."

"What have you done with them? Sold them second hand down the Harbour Road?"

"No, of course I have not. What do you take me for? I have given them dowries and found them husbands."

"And when you get tired of me, will you give me a dowry and find me a husband?"

"Stella, what are you talking about? Don't be so silly."

"Or shall I have to sell myself in the Harbour Road?"

"Stella, I will kill you if you talk like this. I am not a white man."

"And I am not a yellow woman. You will be called to account if you kill me."

"Did you tell any one you were coming here?"

"No."

"Well, I didn't, you may be quite sure of that. Who is going to call me to account if I kill you, Stella?"

"Why do you want to kill me if you say you love me?"

"It is a little way we have in this country when our love af-

100

fairs go wrong."

"And you think it improves a love affair to kill the girl?"

"It stops the pain, Stella."

"And you think that as soon as I am out of the way, you will be able to console yourself?"

"Oh no, I never said that. I said there is no pain in death. Come, shall we burn the house down? It would burn like tinder."

He took a box of matches out of his pocket, and began to strike them and throw them about the dusty room.

"Don't be crazy, Wu Lu," cried Stella, rushing after them and putting her foot on them. "What about poor old Wang?"

"Oh, let him run out like a rat, what does it matter?"

He threw a match into a dusty cotton curtain, and the flame ran up it in a swift yellow tongue. Stella sprang at it and tore it down and stamped on it.

"Oh, Wu Lu, don't carry on like this! It is perfectly daft. If this place once catches alight, it will burn in good earnest."

"I am in good earnest. Did you think I was playing?" Oh, damn, that is the last of my matches. Never mind, there are other ways. Tell me, Stella, do you love me or not?"

"Not if you behave like this, I don't. I think you're a perfect nuisance. I'm going home."

"Oh no, you aren't."

"Why not?"

"Because I'm between you and the door."

"Wu Lu, do you mean—?"

"Yes, I do!"

Stella charged straight at him where he stood blocking the narrow space between the end of Wang's coffin and the wall; but instead of crashing into his arms, as he expected, she took one clean bound and cleared the coffin—no mean feat—and went flying down the rickety staircase helter-skelter, shaking the whole house in her flight. She flashed one searing look at Wang as she rushed through the shop, and then away she went down the crowded street, leaving him blinking behind his horners.

CHAPTER IX

STELLA flung herself on her bed, completely overcome. But the thing that had collapsed her was not the danger she had been in, for she had not realised that till the last moment, but the shock and disillusionment of the dishonourable offer Li had made her. Over and over again she asked herself:

"What have I done that he dared make me such an offer?"

It had never entered her head that any one could suggest anything to her except marriage. It was unbelievable. So far as she knew, there had never been a scandal in her family. Honourable, clean-living, simple gentlefolk, such a thing was unthinkable in connection with them. Even if Li had set the house on fire, as he very nearly had, she would not have yielded to him.

But one thing was quite certain—she loved him desperately, loved him passionately; the extraordinary scene with him had stirred depths in her she had never known existed. She knew now why he had called her a baby, an unborn child; she understood now, for the first time, what he must have been feeling towards her behind his mask of calm.

"If he's got half the heartache I have, I'm sorry for him," thought Stella.

Oblivious of the passage of time, she lay exhausted with her grief, till at length her aunt came to see what had become of her.

"Stella, are you never going to get up? My goodness, child, you do look like the morning after the night before What did you drink?"

"Flat champagne," said Stella.

"How much of it?"

"I don't know."

"No, I don't suppose you do. Well, you'd better have a cold shower and some salts."

Stella crept down, not knowing what the time might be, and came into the pre-lunch cocktail-drinking. She was received with a barrage of chaff about her hang-over, till even Mr. Hope took pity on her.

"Leave her alone," he said. "If you've ever had a head yourself, you'd be sorry for her. I think this is one of the rare cases when a hair of the dog that bit you is indicated. What did you drink, Stella?"

"Champagne," said Stella miserably and untruthfully.

"Then you had better have a glass of that; salts aren't going to meet your case. I daresay we could all do with a drop of it. What do you say, Florence?"

"I certainly could," said Mrs. Hope, who had got just as bad a hang-over as Stella, only being used to it, she was carrying it better.

Then everybody had another laugh at the way Stella revived under the influence of the champagne, attributing her rapid recovery to the excellence of her liver, little knowing that the girl they were chaffing so heartily about her supposed Bacchanalian exploits had just been within an ace of being burnt alive by a sex-crazed Chinaman.

They all sat limply round, their glasses in their hands, paying interest on John Barleycorn's mortgage. It was a great surprise to Stella that they seemed to think nothing of it that a girl should get dead drunk at a party, as they believed her to have done; for Mrs. Hope had told with great gusto of having found Stella on her bed fully dressed, even to her shoes—she herself being too muzzy with her own hang-over to have observed that Stella was in street costume and not in evening dress.

Then, as so often happened in the circles in which the Hopes moved, Li's name came up.

"Damn the man!" thought Stella, "Am I never to get away from him?"

"Li's on the razzle again," said some one. "He's cut all his appointments to-day, including our shareholders' meeting.

Can't get hold of him, and can't do anything with him. His right-hand man's pretty flustered, too, I could tell that, even on the telephone."

"I expect his new concubine's playing him up," said Rosemary with a great air of worldly wisdom. Stella, who had been brought up not to refer to such things, stared at her, startled. Then she remembered that she herself had had a great deal to say on the subject of concubines to the owner of them, and her sense of humour came to the rescue.

"Has Li got a new concubine?" asked some one else.

So Rosemary says," said her father. "I don't know who is her authority for the statement."

"I don't know either," said Rosemary, "unless it was Stella."

"I'm sure it wasn't!" cried Stella horrified, thinking that her secret was about to be discovered.

"Look at her blushing!" giggled Rosemary.

"And quite right too" said her father. "Nice girls don't talk about concubines. Stella has been well brought up, which is more than can be said for you, young woman."

"Quite nice girls are concubines nowadays," said Rosemary, helping herself to the dregs of the champagne, and Stella felt herself getting still redder. They little knew how near the mark their random arrows were flying.

"Talking about Li," said Mr. Mathers, who as usual had dropped in at the cocktail hour, "you ought to keep an eye on that amah of yours."

Wild guffaws greeted this remark.

"No, I don't mean what you mean," said the journalist. "But the windows of the editorial sanctum overlook the back door of the I. and 0. Bank, and I see all Li's secret service coming and going, and she's one of them. Comes every week for her little bit, and has for some time now. I knew she was some one's amah, but didn't know whose; but I saw her hanging around the ladies' cloakroom at your party, and I recognised her."

"We'd better sack her," said Mrs. Hope.

"Not the slightest use," said Mr. Hope, "he'd only corrupt

the next one, if that's his game. If a Chinaman makes up his mind to spy on you, you've got to put up with it. I'm glad of the hint, all the same, Mathers. I'll be dashed careful with my papers. I wonder what in the world Li's playing at?"

"That is a thing which no man knows," said Mr. Mathers, rising to go. "I shouldn't be surprised if Li didn't even know himself, he's being so erratic these days."

But Stella knew, and her heart missed a beat. So Li had been employing the amah to spy upon her? She was pretty certain that was the explanation; if he had been on the track of Mr. Hope's secrets, he would have employed one of the menservants, who had access to his belongings, instead of the amah, who had nothing to do with any one save the women of the family.

Her worst fears were confirmed when she went up to bed and found the amah ostensibly tidying her room, a thing she had never done before, and was not expected to do, having her hands quite full enough with the keg-meg of Mrs. Hope and Rosemary.

Stella, nerves on edge, was about to pounce on her and charge her with treachery, when in a voice hardly louder than a breath, she said: Honourable virgins should be careful, very careful. There are bad men about—kidnappers—"

Stella, her heart almost stopping, sat down helplessly on the foot of the bed. Kidnapping is an ever-present menace hanging over the heads of any one of substance in China, and women have more to fear from kidnappers than men. Moreover, Stella dared not go to her uncle for protection, for to do so would involve the whole ugly story coming out, and get Li into very serious trouble. The amah, never raising her eyes, finished her imaginary job and drifted out of the room like a shadow.

This was the second time Stella had been warned by one of Li's creatures to look out for trouble with him. What strange beings the Chinese were. There was dear old Wang, a good old man if ever there was one, calmly lending a hand at a seduction; and there was the amah, drawing her weekly wage as a spy; yet both of them risked everything to give her a word of warning; what they risked, Stella knew for herself from the state into which she had seen Li get his cuffs.

Then there was Li himself—a collection of contradictions, so far as she could see, every trait he possessed being matched by its opposite. Amazing self-control, followed by a lunatic out-burst. Extraordinarily gentle and considerate, and then, after seeing her safely home, going back and spending the rest of the night torturing some one, and getting his shirt-cuffs all dabbled in blood.

And he, on his side, must have been just as bewildered by her, she thought. After allowing herself to develop an intim-acy with him never dreamt of by the women of his race, and showing her feelings, even if involuntarily, in a way unheard of among them, she had suddenly developed an acute attack of virtue when he drew the—to him—obvious conclusions from her conduct.

And then there was this threat of kidnapping. Stella sitting on the foot of the bed, staring out into the moonless night, felt a cold shudder run down her spine as she thought of it. Li, wrong side out, was a dangerous brute. Then she suddenly realised that the curtains were not drawn. With all her tidying, the amah had not performed the obvious service of drawing the curtains. Mr. Hope, like all people who live in countries where shooting is a commonplace, was very particular that the blinds should always be drawn before the lights were switched on. It was a habit that had soon been drummed into Stella by the shrieks of horror her disregard of it called forth. It was one of the few things the stolid Rosemary was frightened of—the lighted lamp and the undrawn blind.

Stella felt herself beginning to tremble. Should she turn out the light before she drew the blind, or should she risk draw-ing the blind with the light on? Then she tried to pull herself together. Li would not kill if he meant to kidnap, she told her-self. He wanted her alive, not dead. She went over to the win-dow and boldly drew the blind. Then she sank back on the bed again, the perspiration running down her.

In that warm climate they slept with their doors open to get all the air there was; but to-night Stella closed and bolted hers. Then she looked doubtfully at the window. Could she bear to sleep with it shut? She decided that she could not, and content-ed herself with arranging all the toilette crockery on the sill and under it as a trap for intruders. Then she got into bed and lay listening to every sound. There was a night-watchman, but she had no faith in him, knowing what she did of the faithlessness of the amah; if Li could corrupt the one, he could corrupt the other.

Then she fell asleep and dreamed, and her dreams were full of fear and distress; but in her dreams she did not fear Li, but was looking for him, wandering through all the public rooms of a big hotel where he was supposed to be stopping. And finally she saw him sitting at a table in the lounge, drinking tea, and she went up to him, ever so happy and relieved to see him; and then, before he could speak to her, she woke up—and wept for a while because she knew it was a dream which could never come true. But somehow, after that dream, she had less fear and felt calmer; and something in her, which she would never have admitted by daylight was there, felt that to be kidnapped by Li would not be unrelieved tragedy. But something else replied that that was an adventure which could only end in one place—the Harbour Road, where that night from the tram she had seen the poor harpies plying their dreadful trade. In her mind ran a couplet from the verse of the Poet of Empire so much disliked by Mr. Li:

> *"When a man is tired, there is naught that will bind him;*
> *All he ever promised he will put behind him."*

Then, towards dawn, she slept fitfully again, and woke late to face a world that seemed liable at any moment to explode in her face.

The days dragged by, and the strain told on Stella, On two occasions Mrs. Hope's little dog woke in the night and indulged in a hurricane of barks, and Stella made quite sure that Li's thugs were closing in on the house.

The family remarked on her weary looks.

"By Jove, Stella, you've hobnailed your liver properly," said her uncle, eying her sharply. " If she doesn't pull up soon, Florence, you had better get the doctor to her."

"Nonsense, she doesn't need a doctor. Stella's crossed in love, what's what the matter with her," snapped Mrs. Hope, whose own liver left much to be desired at the moment. Mr. Hope raised his eyebrows at Stella, who, suddenly losing her self-control, burst into tears and rushed from the table.

'Who's the gent?" she heard him enquire as she crossed the hail, and to her relief heard her aunt reply: "One of her father's contemporaries, I gather."

After that things were easier for her, and there was considerably more tolerance for her, both in the house and among the Hopes' friends, so she gathered that that story had spread, But she did not mind; it was first-class cover for her real trouble. She was horrified, however, to find that her self-control was so fragile, and dreaded that she might betray herself under conditions whose significance would be unmistakable.

Then it began to be noticed that she was no longer going to Mr. Wang's as she had been doing, and she was cross questioned on the subject. Luckily for her, her nerves had steadied somewhat by that time, and she was able to give a good account of herself. She had been warned, she said, that things were unsettled in Chinatown, and she had better keep away till further notice.

"That confirms what I have suspected for some time," said Mr. Mathers, who, being the tame cat about the house, was present when the subject had come up for discussion.

"Li is brewing something. He's stopped all deals and cleared out to his place at Pei-Chi. He seems to be doing a kind of retreat."

"Much more likely getting over a binge as bad as Stella's," said Mr. Hope. "I heard at the club that he went in there the night after our dance and absolutely raised hell till McCulloch got him away. Said he hated all foreigners—China for the Chinese—and ail that sort of nonsense. Drunk as an owl."

"No, Robert, you're wrong, he wasn't drunk, that's just the trouble. He was as near running amok as a man can be and not get his knife out. I've talked to one or two fellows who were there. He had them scared stiff. They thought he was going to shoot the place up. If Li's taking that tack—rounding on Europeans, it's going to be nasty."

"Nonsense, the fellow was drunk. There's no need to take him seriously. I've seen Li go in off the deep end before and talk the hind leg off a jackass, all about nothing."

Nearly a fortnight had gone by since she had broken with Li; Stella had got over the acute stage of her distress and had settled down into apathy and utter distaste for life. The family got used to her silence and her weary looks and took them as a matter of course, going on as usual with their routine of the rather limited pleasure afforded by the commercial society of the treaty port in which they lived and moved and had their being. The Hopes were the leading lights among the moneyed business folk, but there was also a social circle of the diplomats that considered itself a cut above commerce and had no truck with it, save when charities were concerned. Stella, surveying them and their womenfolk from a distance at the pony-races and other conglomerate gatherings, thought that she would have been much happier if her lot had been cast among those who served their country's interests rather than those who served their own,

But the social round was to undergo a temporary suspension, despite Rosemary's outspoken disgust; a Mr. and Mrs. Little, Philadelphia Quakers, were expected as visitors for a few days, and one could hardly take them to the races or entertain them with bridge. They had to be shown the sights and introduced to the important people because Mr. Little's son was the head of a firm of shippers that handled all the American business of the Hope Navigation Co., and it was very desirable that they should be impressed with the probity, standing and general efficiency of Robert Hope. Quakers are cute, and their standards are high, and Mr. Hope had no wish that an unfavourable report should reach one of his most important business connections; therefore for the week preceding the arrival of the Littles, he knocked off all alcohol and lived almost exclusively on soda-mints and lime juice, a curious combination that Stella expected to see explode inside him; his temper, never of the sweetest, suffered in consequence, and Rosemary was subject to a barrage of instructions concerning deportment, language and choice of garments, which caused her temper, which was not of the sweetest either, to suffer proportionately; she passed on the kick to Stella, till Mrs. Hope intervened and said it would not do to let the Littles, who, being Quakers, might have ideals on the subject of the treatment of poor relations—see Stella being bullied, and bade her restrain herself. Finally, just as the Littles were actually expected, Mr. Hope gave a final word of admonition:

"Now look here, you girls, there is not to be a word about Li's binge, or the unrest in the Chinese quarter, or anything. You understand that, do you, Rosemary and Stella?"

Rosemary snorted. "What do I care about Li's binges? I'm not his mother. I only talk about them because they're amusing."

"They won't be amusing to Mr. Little, who knows we're practically in his hands. He won't like that sort of thing, being a Quaker."

"Damn the Quakers," said Rosemary, who had been told that she must not swear during the Quaker visitation.

"You understand too, Stella?"

"Yes, Uncle Robert; but they won't be wanting to go down Chinatown, will they? Because I'd much sooner not go down there as things are at present."

"No, they won't want to go there. We'll tell them there's smallpox about."

Then the car drew up at the door, and two small, stout people, like a pair of grey pigeons, got out.

Stella liked the Littles the moment she set eyes on them.

Homely, kindly and genuine, she felt them to be; no frills, but sterling friends to those to whom they gave their friendship. She wondered what they would make of Esperanza House; it was the last place to which to bring Quakers in the ordinary way, but its glories had been drastically dimmed for the occasion.

Although, for the benefit of the Littles, Mrs. Hope was honey itself to Stella, Mrs. Little, who had her full share of the unworldly shrewdness of the Quakers, had not been in the house twenty-four hours before she spotted that something was very much amiss with the orphan niece, and being a motherly soul, tried to draw her out and win her confidence; but without success, for Stella's trouble was not one that could be confided; and Mrs. Little reluctantly abandoned her efforts when she found the girl securely barricaded behind a wall of silence and aloofness.

The first day of their stay the Littles had been shown the readily available sights within the Concession, and Stella's services had not been required; the second day there was a reception in their honour that started at four in the afternoon as an At Home, and ended up as a full-dress dinner in the evening, to which festivities Mrs. Little responded with suitable variations of her Quaker grey, looking more like a pigeon than ever, and quite unmoved by all the festivities. The only thing that moved her to admiration was Stella's frock, of which she approved highly. Rosemary, who received no compliment of any sort, snorted and tossed her head and made disparaging remarks on Quaker taste behind the visitors' backs.

The third day was employed in a trip in a launch up the coast, in which Stella was not included owing to the limited accommodation; and then the fourth day there befell what she had been so greatly fearing all along—one of the motoring picnics into the interior that were such a popular feature of Concession junketings in that warm climate. It was just the opportunity for a kidnapping, if that were what Li had in his mind. The previous evening maps had been got out, and the route decided on, and all plans made in the hearing of the servants. Stella, sitting silently beside her aunt as she pored over the map, considered the chosen route carefully, and decided that if she were staging a kidnapping, there was one particular place where she would stage it—a narrow glen that led up to a pass where a particularly good view was to be obtained. From that glen a road led away into the heart of the tangled hilly country that lay behind the coast. Studying the map, she also saw that it was possible to over-shoot the turning and keep to a broad level road along the river valley, thickly strewn with villages, where a hold-up would be out of the question. There was, of course, no view worth mentioning on that route, and it would be thick with carts and children and chickens and dust, but it would be as safe as anything was, outside the barbed wire of the Concession. Stella made up her mind that she would brave her aunt's wrath and overshoot that turning.

Despite their laudable intentions of an early start, the Hopes as usual got off for their picnic pretty late. Rosemary, Mrs. Hope and Mrs. Little sat behind in the spacious back of the tonneau, and Mr. Little sat with Stella in front. Although Stella considered the particular glen she had noted as the ideal spot for a hold-up, there were plenty of places on the road that would have served nearly as well. For a considerable distance after leaving the Concession she had to follow the route as originally planned, and her heart was beating hard as she came to a spot where she knew a hold-up to be feasible. Accelerating suddenly, she swung round the corner hooting violently, taking her chance of what might be on the other side, and went tearing off in a cloud of dust as if the devil were after her. Mrs. Hope, always a nervous motorist, shrieked at her to be careful.

At the next bend she repeated her manoeuvre, very nearly abolishing a mule-team and driver. The road climbed in a series of hairpin bends, and at every one Stella did a sprint. It was a hair-raising performance, and Mrs. Hope was nearly demented, screaming at Stella like an angry parrot, entirely forgetting the presence of the Littles, who had got to be favourably impressed. They, for their part, sat with stoical Quaker calm, enduring both Stella's driving and Mrs. Hope's screaming as best they might.

"I think Stella's gone balmy," said Rosemary philosophically.

"She's gone nothing of the sort," cried Mrs. Hope angrily, "she's just doing it to annoy."

"Hi, Stella! You've overshot the turning!" yelled Rosemary.

"Stella!" screeched Mrs. Hope. "That's the turning for the Pass—on the left—you've just passed it."

Stella took no notice. Mrs. Hope rose from her seat and hammered her between the shoulders with her clenched fist, causing a violent swerve.

"Hi, Mummy, sit down! " cried Rosemary, "you'll wreck the whole shoot," and she pulled the almost hysterical Mrs. Hope back into her seat.

"STELLA! " she yelled in a stentorian voice that was not to be ignored. "STOP! Mummie wants you to stop!"

Stella, having gained the widening valley, had no objection to stopping now, and slid to a standstill in the midst of a village.

In an instant the car was surrounded by a milling mob of children and beggars, stinking, verminous, diseased—begging alms and shouting abuse. Some one threw a fish-head, which Rosemary hastily pitched back.

"Drive on, Stella!" gasped Mrs. Hope, leaning back in her seat, quite overcome. Stella drove on.

Now there was no need to fear a hold-up she drove more rationally, and although the drive was hot, dusty and smelly, it was no longer nerve-racking. Mrs. Hope began to recover her equanimity and to remember it was desirable to impress the Littles favourably, which was not likely to be done if they heard them all screaming at each other in family tiffs. She put Stella's delinquency aside, to be dealt with at a more convenient season, and began to chat pleasantly to her guests, gradually raising her own spirits as she did so, till by the time the car turned onto the coast road and was back again among beautiful scenery, she was quite restored, and her usual chatty and charming social self.

"There's a lovely place to have lunch along here," she cried. "I'm sure you must all be simply starving."

As it was nearly three o'clock everybody admitted they were.

Stella, nothing loath, being now out of the danger zone and in a spot far from their original route, ran the car down a cart-track through a little wood of stone-pines, out onto a headland. On either side the coast stretched away in a series of loops, bay succeeding bay as rocky spurs ran down to the sea from the main range. The sand was almost silver in its whiteness; the sea almost indigo in its blueness; trees clothed the slopes along which the coast road was carried on a graded ledge, following the contours of the spurs; it was impossible to imagine a greater contrast with the marshy, smelly, over-populated valley down which they had just come.

"Dear me," said Mr. Little, as he sat down beside the picnic cloth spread on the short turf," this is the first time I have seen real woods in this part of the world."

"Yes, the deforestation is deplorable, it has quite changed the climate," said Mrs. Hope, "These woods belong to a friend of ours, Li Wu Lu; you may have heard your son speak of him."

"Do they really? Yes, of course I have heard of Mr. Li. I should very much like to meet him while I am here, if it is possible. My son has a very high opinion of him. In fact, he is greatly in his debt." And he proceeded to tell a rather long-winded tale of an occasion when Li had stood by a verbal agreement to his own detriment.

Stella, listening with an impassive face turned out to sea, was somehow made happier by learning that Li's reputation stood so high among people whose opinion she felt to be well worth having.

"Of course you shall meet him," said Mrs. Hope impulsively. She was rather proud of what she believed to be her intimacy with the Chinese millionaire, and liked showing it off. "I had hoped he would turn up at our At Home; he often does; he was at our dance the other night. We will ask him in one evening while you are here. He is really very charming. If it wasn't for his face, you would think he was a white man. He is a very old friend of ours, you know. We have known him ever since he came back from Oxford to take charge of the bank when his father died so suddenly. Robert helped him a great deal in those days; it was a very trying position for an inexperienced boy to be thrust into, and he has never forgotten it."

"Oh?" said Mr. Little. "Was he as young as all that when he took charge?"

"Oh yes, he was only just down from Oxford. He is still in the early thirties, even now."

"You surprise me," said Mr. Little; "he has done some very remarkable work for his age."

"Yes, he is a very remarkable man. Robert has a very high opinion of him."

"I have always heard him spoken of extremely highly," said Mr. Little.

A muffled snigger came from Rosemary. Her mother frowned at her.

"It's an ant running up my leg," said Rosemary, turning away and scratching herself with unnecessary vigour.

"What is that building out on the next point?" asked Mrs. Little, pointing across the perfect crescent of the bay that lay below them to where the red peaked roofs of Chinese architecture showed among the trees of another headland.

Mrs. Hope, who was short-sighted, adjusted her lorgnette and gazed at them.

"Why, that's Li's house, Pei-Chi," she said. "I had no idea we were so close. We'll call on him on our way back. He'll be delighted to see us, he's a very old friend of ours. I should love you to see a genuine Chinese garden, and his is a perfect marvel; and his collection of Chinese art—well, you admired mine, but you ought to see his."

Stella's heart stood still, frozen within her.

"I shouldn't if I were you," she said. "You heard Uncle say that Mr. Li had been doing a kind of retreat or something."

Rosemary guffawed, and pretended to hunt for another ant.

"Nonsense," said Mrs. Hope, looking angrily from one girl to the other. "He'll have got over that long ago," as if a retreat were some sort of complaint.

Stella, knowing the uselessness of protest, and unable to

give her real reasons, determined that she would again play the trick of driving fast and over-shooting the turning.

Sitting on the short turf of the headland waiting for her aunt to finish her after-lunch cigarette, Stella gazed down onto the roofs of Li Wu Lu's home, and wondered what vultures were gnawing at his soul on the rock to which he had betaken himself. Even from that distance she could see that the house was a blend of European and Chinese architecture, skilfully combined; the roofs preserving the traditional tent-shaped outline in all its coloured beauty, but underneath their broad eaves European windows let in light and air. Mr. Li knew how to make the best of both civilisations.

He had often talked to her about that house, to which he was devoted. Both it and its gardens he had designed himself, making of them a work of art, bringing back treasures for them from his overseas trips. In fact, it was from his over flowing collection that Mr. Wang's shop had originated. He had half suggested more than once that he would like to take her out to see Pei-Chi, if it could be managed without compromising either of them. But it never appeared possible to do that, and so the visit had never come off.

Forgetful of her companions, Stella sat gazing down onto her friend's house with an aching heart, wondering how it was faring with him. She felt pretty certain that it was faring badly. She knew that since their break he had attended to no business, and that his last appearance in public had been on the occasion when he had made a scene at the club. For the party of them to turn up at his house in the family Daimler and demand tea was a grotesque nightmare, so grotesque that she could hardly believe it could possibly happen.

In fact, it was more than grotesque, it was highly dangerous. Li in his present mood would be capable of anything. She certainly would not escape with her honour, and the others would be exceedingly lucky if they escaped with their lives. The more she thought of it, the more she saw its ugly possibilities, and she determined that all costs she must prevent the visit to Pei-Chi, even if it involved some pretty plain speaking.

With her heart beating and her hands trembling she started up the car and took it back onto the road. She would overshoot the turning if she could, that would be her first line of defence. But she had reckoned without the windings of the coast road; to drive fast here was simply suicidal. Consequently the Daimler came nosing slowly round a bend and brought them face to face with a signboard announcing the way to Pei-Chi in both Chinese and European characters. There was no getting away from it.

"There you are, Stella," called Mrs. Hope. "Turn down here."

Stella set her teeth and drove on.

"Stella!" Mrs. Hope's voice cut icily across the comparative quiet of the slowly-moving car. "Will you stop a moment, please?"

Stella stopped. That was a request that could not very well be ignored. Moreover, if they were to argue the matter out, it was better to do it while stationary than to risk going over the cliff-edge through her attention being distracted. She brought the car to a standstill, but did not turn round in her seat.

"Stella," came Mrs. Hope's voice again, icy cold and with an edge on it. "Will you kindly back the car and turn down to the left and drive to Pei-Chi, where I wish to call on Mr. Li?"

"I shouldn't, if I were you, Aunt Florence," said Stella unemotionally.

"Will you kindly do as I ask?"

"I think it is very unwise, Aunt Florence."

"Who do you suppose knows best, I who have spent all my life in this country, or you who have only been here a few months?

"I do, because I speak the language and mix with the people, and you don't."

"I never heard of such nonsense, you foolish child," said Mrs. Hope, controlling herself with difficulty for the sake of the Littles. "Do as I ask you, and don't behave in this ridiculous manner. You are spoiling the whole trip."

"Please don't go on our account, Mrs. Hope," intervened

Mr. Little. "We can meet Mr. Li some other time, it really is of no importance."

"Of course we are going, there is absolutely no reason why we shouldn't. Stella, drive there at once, and let us have no more of this nonsense," exclaimed Mrs. Hope, her temper getting the better of her self-restraint.

"No, Aunt Florence, I will not drive you there. It is too risky."

"My dear Stella, don't be ridiculous. What are you afraid of?"

Stella paused a moment, and then she said: "I am afraid of being murdered."

"My darling child, don't be so absolutely absurd. Li is one of our oldest friends. Now come along, Stella, are you going to do as I tell you?"

"No," said Stella. "If you choose to risk it, you can come some other time when I am not here, but that is a risk I am just not going to take."

"Please don't press the matter, Mrs. Hope," said Mr. Little. "We should really feel most unhappy to go if Miss Stella feels so strongly about it."

"It is simply too childish!" cried Mrs. Hope, "Li is a great friend of ours. He'll be delighted to see us, we have a standing invitation; he runs in and out of our house as if he were one of the family. We have been to Pei-Chi dozens of times. Stella, stop this hysterical nonsense and drive there at once."

Stella did not answer.

"Stella, as long as you are in my house, I expect you to respect my wishes. If you do not respect my wishes, you will cease to remain in my house."

There was dead silence for a moment, then Stella spoke, and her voice, too, had a cutting edge on it.

"I see—the bread of charity must be earned by obedience?"

"Precisely," said Mrs. Hope tartly.

"All right, I'll earn it," said Stella.

"Mrs. Hope, I beg of you—not on our account—" began

Mr. Little, very troubled, but they neither of them took any notice of him. Stella engaged the gears in reverse, and the big car began to move slowly backwards; it came to the lane to Pei-Chi; she turned its nose down, and the Rubicon was passed. They ran on slowly over a well-kept surface till the way was barred by heavy gates, handsomely carved, with a gateman's hut beside them.

The sound of their wheels on the gravel brought the gate-man out, clad in clean blue cotton garments with the great scarlet Li crest on his back. Mrs. Hope waved a dollar bill under his nose and demanded in pidgin that his master should be informed of their presence. The gate-man looked longingly at the dollar bill, but replied in the same dreadful argot that his orders left him no discretion: his honourable master was not receiving. Mrs. Hope produced a second bill, but the gate-man was adamant. She might bribe, but his master would kill, and kill unpleasantly, and she could not bid against that.

"No can do," he said with a sigh, looking regretfully at the bills fluttering in the breeze. Then his eyes met Stella's, and she recognised him as a man she had several times seen come into Wang's with messages. He gave no sign of recognition, and neither did she, but he immediately put out his hand for the dollar bills. Mrs. Hope gave him one, but kept hold of the other, and he disappeared through the little side gate in the direction of the house.

CHAPTER X

HE kept them waiting so long that they began to think had he made off with the dollar with no intention of returning, but just as Mrs. Hope was on the verge of giving Stella instructions to turn the car and drive away, they heard a sound of heavy bolts being withdrawn, and the carved gates swung slowly back, revealing a winding drive bordered with the most exquisite flowering shrubs, great tree-peonies bearing hundreds of blooms of every conceivable shade from white to damson, through pink, fuchsia and crimson. It was a breath taking sight, and everybody exclaimed at it—everybody except Stella, and she sat in the driving-seat as if frozen, driving mechanically, unable to feel her hands. The gateman, travelling with them on the running-board, appeared to be in high feather.

Rounding the last curve of the drive, they came out onto a broad expanse of gravel where a car could turn easily; at the far side a wide flight of shallow stone steps led up to a low terrace guarded against evil spirits by ferocious stone lions. Framed in the beautiful caved doorway of the house stood a dignified figure in plain coolie blue, slowly waving an ivory fan. It did not advance to meet them.

Stella brought the car to a standstill alongside the steps, and everybody except herself got out.

"Are you coming, Stella?" said Mrs. Hope coldly.

"No, I'll wait here," said Stella. Mrs. Hope turned her back on her and led the others up the steps. Still Li did not advance to meet them, but stood in his doorway slowly waving his fan and awaiting their coming. Stella, who knew her etiquette, saw that they were being received as a Chinese receives those who are very much his inferiors. Mrs. Hope, who ought to have known it, appeared to notice nothing. The Littles, of course, had no realisation that they were being insulted about as grossly as it was possible to insult them.

Mrs. Hope sailed up to that silent figure in its plain coolie blue gown of fine silk, and held out her hand.

"Mr. Li," she said, "I have brought our friends, Mrs. and Mr. Little, to see you. I think you know Mr. Little's son, Mr. George Little, of San Francisco."

The motionless blue figure ignored the outstretched hand, and continuing slowly to wave the ivory fan, looked them over with a totally unrecognising stare. Then he barked one word.

The gate-man leapt forward as if kicked from behind and flung himself flat on his face on the ground at his master's feet.

Li barked a brief question at him.

The gate-man whimpered a reply, pointing towards the car.

Li, ignoring his visitors and his prostrate servant, went striding across the terrace in a very un-Chinese manner, his silk skirts flapping behind him. He came to a halt beside the Daimler, rested both hands on the door, and bent down and looked inside.

Stella looked up and saw a mask-like face with two slanting slits for eyes and a mouth shut like a rat-trap, and felt herself go numb with terror.

"Will not the honourable lady alight?" said Li, in exceedingly chi-chi English.

Stella shook her head.

"Oh, but I beg of the honourable lady to alight. The spirits of my ancestors will be affronted."

Stella looked up at him appealingly.

"No," she said in a low voice.

"Yes," said Li, and opening the door he reached inside, took her by the arm and dragged her out. Unable to get her balance on the step, she fell full on his chest. Clutching him as she scrambled for her balance, she could feel his heart hammering through the thin silk, and to her nostrils came once again the faint sweet spicy odour of the sandalwood chest in which he kept his clothes, and it was all China to her. As she struggled to her feet, her handbag fell to the ground with a thud that betokened it contained something heavy.

"Hein?" said Li, and stooped and picked it up. He did not hand it back to her.

"The honourable lady will honour my poor house?" said Li in a loud voice in his chi-chi English, obviously for the benefit of the onlookers, who stood staring, not quite knowing what was afoot. The Littles were alarmed and offended by the rough handling of Stella, but seeing that Mrs. Hope took it as a matter of course, concluded that they had better do likewise. Rosemary was openly agape; Mrs. Hope was more uneasy than she chose to admit, even to herself, seeing plainly that Li was by no means back to normal after his alleged binge and that Stella had been perfectly right in not wanting to visit him.

"Will the honourable lady enter my poor house?" said Li again, as Stella stood staring helplessly up into his face that looked like an evil yellow mask, resembling in an extra ordinary manner the countenance of the god of war and pestilence in Mr. Wang's shop. "Have I any choice?" she said in a low voice.

"None."

"Then let me turn off the petrol. You won't like it if it overflows and your house goes on fire."

"Would you mind if my poor house went on fire?"

"Very much — if I were on the premises when it happened."

Li suddenly laughed, and his laugh sounded comparatively natural. It was with just such remarks as this that Stella used to amuse him at the tea-rituals. He turned and walked towards the party waiting before his door, Stella's hand-bag clasped in one hand and her wrist in the other.

"Shall we go in?" he said in perfectly normal English, waving them towards the door with the hand that held Stella's bag. Stella saw Mrs. Little staring at the hand that held her wrist, and hoped to heaven she would have the tact to keep quiet.

Once inside the beautiful tiled entrance hall, Li let go of Stella's wrist, though he still kept tight hold of her bag, and led his visitors into a kind of loggia, its ends banked high with flowering plants in great porcelain pots and its arches glassed in against the sea-breeze.

"Pray be seated," he said bowing ceremonially, "while I go to give instructions for your refreshment."

He disappeared, and Stella, who knew that no Chinese grandee ever goes to speak to his servants, but always summons them with gong or hand-clap, wondered what mischief he was brewing, That they would not get out of his house without very serious trouble, she was quite certain.

"Oh, I say, look what I've found!" exclaimed Rosemary, pulling forward from behind a plant a tray containing an elaborate outfit for smoking opium.

"Goodness me! Li of all people," exclaimed Mrs. Hope.

"The head and front of the anti-opium campaign!"

"I say, this will raise a laugh!" said Rosemary.

"It will raise more than a laugh," said Mrs. Hope.

"Don't you think," came Stella's voice in cold tones, "that if you see a thing like that when you are a guest in a house, you are honour bound to keep quiet about it?"

"My dear Stella, don't be so self-righteous. This is a very important piece of information."

"Well," said Stella, "you wouldn't like it if I broadcast how much Uncle drinks, which I have seen while I have been in your house."

"My dear Stella—! How can you say such a thing!"

"I shall broadcast it if you talk about Mr. Li's opium."

Mrs. Hope opened her mouth to slay Stella, then looked up and saw Li standing beside her.

"Hein?" he said. "Shall we sit down?"

Mrs. Hope subsided into a cane chair of European manufacture; Li sat down on a kind of high divan, looking as if he were holding a court. His gaze turned slowly and meditatively from one to the other as they sat in a semi-circle in front of him.

"And to what do I owe the honour of this visit?" he said, in his best Oxford English, not a trace of chi-chi in it. Stella

123

wondered what the Littles made of his alternating accents. "We have been showing our friends, Mr. and Mrs. Little, something of China, they are on a world tour, you know; and I was so anxious for them to see your lovely house and garden, and your marvellous collection, so as we were passing, we thought we'd look in and see if you were at home," said Mrs. Hope, speaking as if to a child.

"The botanical gardens at Shanghai are better than my garden," said Li, "and the collection at the South Kensington Museum in London is better than my collection." He turned to Mr. Little.

"Do you know anything of Chinese art?"

"Nothing whatever," said Mr. Little.

"Hein," said Li. "You are at least honest. Tell me, why have you come to see me?"

"I asked Mrs. Hope to bring us because I wished to meet you after having heard my son speak of you. I wished to have the opportunity to thank you for the great service you did him upon a certain occasion."

"Because I honoured an undertaking that could not be en-forced legally? That was not a service to him, it was a service to myself. My own self-respect demanded it. What do I care for your son, Mr. Little? Nothing.

"All the same," he added more gently, "I thank you for your courtesy in visiting me. I am glad it was me you came to see, and not my collection."

His eyes rested for a moment on Mrs. Little, who, grey-gloved hands resting in her plump lap, looked him straight in the eye.

He bowed to her. "My house is honoured by your presence," he said.

She bowed to him. "Your house is very beautiful," she said. Stella, watching them, thought there was something very Chi-nese about the Quakers, and something very Quakerish about the Chinese.

Li's face momentarily lost its mask-like quality.

"I wish you had seen it under happier auspices," he said.

He turned suddenly to Stella.

"And to what do I owe the pleasure of Miss Morris's company?"

Stella looked straight back at him, her head erect, her heart beating.

"To my aunt's command that the bread of charity must be earned by obedience."

"Stella! My dear!" exclaimed Mrs. Hope.

"Hein?" said Li, and raised his eyebrows.

He looked at Stella and she looked back at him with her eyes blazing. There was neither fear nor love in her heart at that moment, only a blind anger against those who were humiliating her—he in one way, and her aunt in another.

"Would you not prefer the rice of friendship to the bread of charity?" said Li with an air of perfect detachment.

"I would," said Stella.

"Hein," said Li, and looked at Mrs. Little.

A servant came in and placed before him a low table bearing the tea-outfit. He looked across at Stella, snapped his fingers at her as if she were a dog, and pointed to the big cushion on the floor by the low tea-table. Stella kicked off her high-heeled shoes, knelt down in front of him, and began the tea-ritual. She heard a gasp from behind her, but she took no notice.

She put out her hand to the delicate china, and as she raised a bowl, she saw that it was the identical one she had used on board ship. She looked up into Li's face, and a rush of tears came to her eyes. She was thankful that her wide Bangkok hat prevented those behind her from seeing her face ; the tears trickled slowly down her cheeks and dried on them; she dared not wipe them away lest she should betray herself to those behind her.

The tea-ritual ran its leisurely course, and when the servant entered to remove the cups, a little, half-grown Pekinese shot in in his wake, rushed up to Stella, and greeted her as an old friend, for he had often been at the tea-parties in the go-down.

"Oh, the dear little fellow!" cried Mrs. Hope, trying to make friends; but Pekinese are exclusive little dogs, and he would have none of her, but stood up in Stella's lap and tried lick her face.

"Little Tsi, you give the show away," said Stella to him, translating the English phrase literally into Chinese, a trick that produced a very comical effect, and that had often served to amuse Li at the tea-parties; it served now, and he laughed again his high Chinese laugh. Stella could feel the party behind her goggling.

She held out her hand towards Li.

"Please may I have my bag?" she said.

"Your bag? Oh, yes, I am sorry. I had forgotten."

He produced the bag out of his voluminous sleeve, weighed it in his hand a moment, and stared at it thoughtfully.

"It is very heavy," he said. "I have always wondered what English ladies carried in these little bags. May I look?" and without waiting for permission, he opened it and took out the little pearl-handed revolver he had given her.

"Hein, Stella," he said, balancing it in his palm and leaning towards her. "Is this for me?"

"No, for me," said Stella quietly.

He looked at her sharply.

"I think I will take care of it," he said, and it disappeared into his sleeve. Then he handed Stella her bag, and she calmly powdered her nose. She could not see the expressions on the faces behind her, but she could sense the steadily rising tension. She knew from the open way Li was handling the situation that he did not mean to let them leave the house alive.

"I think we ought to be moving. It is getting late, and we must be home before dusk," said Mrs. Hope, her voice a trifle quavery.

"But do you not want to see my garden—my collection— that you came to see?" said Mr. Li smoothly.

"I am afraid it is too late for that. It is later than I thought," quavered Mrs. Hope.

"I am sorry," said Li, rising. "I should have liked to have persuaded you to stay and take a meal with me, but, of course, as you say, it is necessary that you should be back before dusk. These roads are very unsafe after dark."

Mrs. Hope heaved a sigh of relief. Li ushered them out of the house, and across the terrace to where the big Daimler stood waiting beside the steps. They made their farewells. They thanked their host. They all got in. Li stood bowing and fanning himself beside the bonnet. Stella pressed the self-starter—and nothing happened. She looked at Li, and Li looked at her out of expressionless eyes. Stella folded her hands in her lap and sat still. That car had been put out of action by a very competent chauffeur, and she wasn't going to waste her time in trying to start it.

Well, Stella, aren't you going to start the car?" said Mrs. Hope impatiently.

"It won't start," said Stella, making no motion.

"Get out and see what's wrong with it," commanded Mrs. Hope.

"No use, I shan't be able to start it."

"You don't know till you try."

"I do know, and I'm not going to make a fool of myself by trying."

"Really, Stella, you are simply too maddening this afternoon. I don't know what's the matter with you. What will Mr. and Mrs. Little think of you, behaving like this?"

"They'll probably think I'm mad," said Stella.

"Mr. Li, could your chauffeur do anything with the car, do you think?—since Stella's so stupid."

"I am sorry, he has taken my car into town to be decarbonised this afternoon. It is most unfortunate. Otherwise I could have sent you home in it."

"Dear, dear, what are we to do? Stella, you've got to do something."

Stella did not stir.

Mr. Little climbed out of the car.

"I do not know very much about cars, but let me see if I can do anything. If it is something simple—" He lifted the bonnet and peered inside.

"It looks to me," he said, "as if your battery had been removed bodily."

"Hein?" said Li, peering into the engine with a fatuous and bird-like air, for which Stella could have smacked him, knowing that he was a very fine driver. "I am afraid I cannot help you. Has your battery fallen off?"

"No," said Stella.

"Been stolen. I expect," said Mr. Little.

"Dear, dear. How very inconvenient. Can't you manage without it ?

"Oh yes, we can manage perfectly if we all get out and shove," said Stella bitterly.

"Stella, be quiet," snapped Mrs. Hope. "Mr. Li, what can we do? Can we get any sort of conveyance to take us home?"

"A bullock cart?" said Li, rubbing his chin thoughtfully.

"How far is it to the Concession?"

"About ten miles."

Mrs. Hope groaned aloud. With diligent goading, a bullock team can do from one and a half to two miles an hour.

"I hesitate to suggest it, but if you would honour me, nothing would give me greater pleasure than to accommodate you for the night; the dusk is already falling, I observe, and you cannot possibly get home by bullock cart before it is dark. I could send a man on horseback with a message to your husband; he would be there in an hour, and he could instruct my chauffeur to bring out a new battery for you when he returns to-morrow with my car."

Mr. Li bowed with the utmost politeness, his face childlike and bland. Stella wondered whether her aunt was taken in. It would have been just like Mrs. Hope's complete self-satisfaction to take what she was told at its face value. Batteries were always being stolen from unattended cars by economical Chinese who wanted replacements for their old flivvers. Of course it was impossible that such a thing should have happened inside Li's compound, where the man who did it would have simply been tossed over the garden wall to the rocks and the sharks, but Mrs. Hope, unbelievably ignorant of the life around her, might not realise that. Stella was furious with Li that he had not taken the trouble to lie more convincingly. He was treating her aunt like a half-wit. Of course she was a half-wit, but Stella felt that in some way it detracted from her own dignity to treat her family so cynically

She looked at her aunt, and to her amazement saw that Mrs. Hope was genuinely delighted at the invitation. Stella knew that her pleasure must be genuine, for she had not got the self-control to have concealed her fear if she had known herself to be in a tight corner. Stella moistened her dry lips with a drier tongue and climbed out of the car with the rest of the party. She looked at the Littles; they were completely self-possessed with the Quaker calm that rivalled Li's own. Entirely ignorant of Chinese life and manners, they were at a disadvantage; danger signals were lost on them that would have cried aloud to any one who knew the country. Nevertheless, they were not fools; Stella could see that they were suspicious, but were pursuing the wise course of masking their suspicions and playing a waiting game. There was nothing anybody could do. If they attempted to make the journey on foot they would be mobbed in the first village, even if Li would be willing to let them go, and if he meant mischief he certainly would not; and if he didn't mean mischief, there was no point in running away at such great inconvenience.

They all trooped back to the house.

"You would no doubt like to refresh yourselves before we dine," said Li. He clapped his hands, and an elderly woman in the dress of a Chinese widow appeared, bowing to every one and smiling most affably. It was obvious to even the least suspicious that she had been awaiting the summons and knew exactly what was expected of her. She collected the women of the party and led them off, while a man-servant escorted Mr. Little in another direction.

Stella had never met her, but she knew who she was—the inevitable poor relation that is to be found in every Chinese household; her job, in the absence of wife or mother, being to supervise the concubines and the women servants generally. Stella wondered how much she knew of Li's goings-on, and what she thought of them.

She was not left long in doubt. The widow looked from Stella to Rosemary and back again, chose Stella, and broke into a torrent of silvery Chinese.

Oh, the heaven-sent relief of her arrival They were all nearly demented. The great lord had been like one distraught. It had been lamentable to see so great a man in such a state, But now that she had come, everything would be all right. Only a little tact was needed. They would all do everything in their power to make her comfortable. She could rest assured that she was more than welcome to the entire household—who, Stella guessed, had been having such a gruelling that they would have welcomed the Devil himself.

Stella replied noncommittally; but in her relief and thankfulness the widow was oblivious of her lack of enthusiasm, and the warmth of her welcome was only second to that of little Tsi, who had stood on his hind-legs and licked her face.

Three beaming little handmaidens came in with ewer and bowl and hand towels, and served Stella first. Fortunately Mrs. Hope was making up at the mirror, and did not notice what was happening, and Mrs. Little, new to China, did not realise the significance that attaches to the simplest acts in a Chinese household. Stella fancied, however, that Mrs. Little was trying to get her apart from the others and have a word with her, and took very good care that she should not manage it.

Their toileting completed, they all returned to the loggia and found Li and Little talking politics in a perfectly rational manner. Then there was the garden to be inspected, a marvel of terraced beauty, some of it formal Chinese, and some of it pure English country house. Then the swift subtropical darkness fell, and they went into a dining-room lit by electricity and took their seats round an English dining table, but the food they ate was pure Chinese.

Li, equally at home in both civilisations, had taken the best of each and blended them without incongruity—no mean achievement.

The food was more than excellent, and Mrs. Little expressed her admiration and asked for recipes; and Mr. Li made himself most agreeable to her, talking of the Chinese cuisine. Then suddenly he glanced across the table and saw that Stella's food lay untouched on her plate. The fears of the others might have been lulled to rest, but she was under no delusion as to what lay before her, and her dry mouth could not swallow the rice.

"Why do you not eat, my child? Don't you like it?" said Li, leaning towards her and speaking perfectly naturally for the first time since they had entered the house, himself forgetting for the moment what was afoot.

Stella shook her head.

"It—it is very nice, thank you, but I just don't want any."

He frowned, leant across, dug his chop-sticks into the mound of flavoured rice in Stella's bowl, picked up a bunch of oddments at random, and ate them. The Littles stared aghast at his manners, not realising what that act signified.

"It isn't that," said Stella. "I just can't manage any."

Her husky voice, hardly under control told him what was amiss with her. He smiled faintly; the eating of fried rice is the Chinese test for a guilty conscience; it is a physical impossibility to swallow it if the mouth is dry with fear.

"Will you drink milk? "he asked.

"Yes, I would like some milk," said Stella.

He gave the order, and a pitcher of rich creamy milk from the famous Pei-Chi Alderneys was brought in. It was borne first to the master of the house. He poured the milk into an egg-shell bowl, drank some, and passed it across to Stella.

"I say, is there a shortage of crockery in this house?" said Rosemary, who had watched these performances with disgust.

"No, there is no shortage of crockery, thank you, we have plenty; but it is a Chinese custom that a guest should not be asked to partake of anything of which the host does not partake himself."

"Is that a precaution against poisoners?" asked Mr. Little, thinking this custom an interesting survival of medievalism, and never dreaming it had any personal application.

"Yes, that is the reason."

"I think I would sooner be poisoned than have some one

drink out of my cup," said Rosemary.

"I wouldn't," said Li. "There is nothing I dislike more than poison."

"But what need is there to drink out of the same cup? Wouldn't it be enough if you had some of the milk in another cup?"

"Would that satisfy you if you were suspicious of me?"

"But Stella wasn't suspicious of you."

"How do you know?"

"Why should she be?"

"You had better ask her that question."

"It looks to me as if you'd got a guilty conscience."

"No, my conscience does not trouble me."

"Is that because it's tough or because it's clear?"

"Rosemary, my dear!" said Mrs. Hope. "You mustn't talk nonsense like this. Mr. Li won't understand it."

"Oh, I understand it perfectly. It does not seem nonsense to me. I think it is very sensible."

"I'm beginning to think it's sensible too," said Rosemary.

"Rosemary, darling, surely you aren't suggesting that Mr. Li is trying to poison us? Why, you know he is one of our oldest friends."

"I wonder," said Rosemary, staring at Li with her bold young eyes.

Li returned the stare. "You are more intelligent than I had taken you to be, Miss Rosemary," he said politely.

"Dear child," gurgled Mrs. Hope, thankful to be able, as she thought, to change the conversation. "Don't let that compliment make you vain. Her boy friends often compliment her on the outside of her head, Mr. Li, but no one has ever complimented her on the inside of it before."

Stella sat listening to this conversation in white-faced horror. She knew, beyond any shadow of doubt, that, whatever was to be her fate, Li did not intend to let the others leave the house alive. She looked across at the Littles, to see what they were making of it, and saw that Mrs. Little was watching her and not the speakers. They looked at each other for a moment. That the little Quakeress was alive to the situation, she could see; but what she made of it, Stella had no means of knowing.

The meal drew to its end, and they set off to perform the solemn farce of inspecting Mr. Li's collection. Stella knew that he was killing time till the hour when his guests could be politely pushed off to bed, and then the real business of the evening would begin.

What did Li mean to do with her? Did he mean to use force? Did he mean to drive a bargain, using the others as hostages? She did not see how he could let them go after having shown his hand so clearly, and in the face of Rosemary's openly expressed suspicions. It seemed to her no injustice that Rosemary and Mrs. Hope should lose their lives at the hands of the Chinese, who they were perpetually abusing, and to whose downfall the business methods of Mr. Hope and his kind had contributed in no small degree; but that the kindly Quaker Littles should be involved in this maelstrom of evil racial passions seemed to her a horror unspeakable.

She looked at Li, playing out the horrible comedy of show- ing his treasures, and thought of the devil that had been un- chained by this tangle of race prejudices in what would other- wise have been a very fine man. She thought of his bitter words concerning the race that had given him a white man's educa- tion but would not allow him a white man's life. Trained as he had been, he could not find happiness with a woman of his own race, and he was not permitted to find happiness with a woman of her race. Unable to settle down, everything that was best in him coming up against insuperable barriers—like a scorpion surrounded by a circle of fire, he was stinging himself to death with his own venom.

She could not see any way out of the present impasse, save in an orgy of destruction and self-destruction. The suspicions of everybody save the nit-witted Mrs. Hope were thoroughly aroused. Stella could not see how, if Li had any care for himself at all, he could dare to let any of them go.

It was an extraordinary dilemma to be in. If she appealed to him to let them go, offering herself as payment, he would be involved in the scandal he had particularly wished to avoid. It was a complete impasse. There only seemed to be one way open to him—to kill the others and keep herself as a prisoner for the rest of her life.

CHAPTER XI

THE weary evening ran its course in the puffing small talk at which Mrs. Hope and Li Wu Lu seemed to be equally good. But in Li's talk there was an undercurrent of innuendo, and Stella wondered how any one who wasn't half-witted could have missed its significance. It was a kind of prose Hymn of Hate. It seemed impossible that any human heart should harbour such intense bitterness and not break with it— perhaps that was what was happening.

Finally they were handed over, with many compliments and politenesses, to the widow hostess to be ushered to their rooms. Smiling, surrounded by her handmaidens, she was enjoying one of the great moments of her life. No suspicion of tragedy had crossed her mind. She probably thought Stella's relations had brought her to the house in due form, and would go away in the morning loaded with presents.

Whatever the rest of the house might be, the bedrooms were pure English, even to the running water and electric radiators. The widow proceeded first to install Mr. and Mrs. Little in a sumptuous apartment with a large double bed, and then to lead the rest of her charges on further. But Mr. Little put his foot down.

"Do you not think it would be better," he said, "if we all kept together?"

"Oh, Mr. Little!" exclaimed Mrs. Hope, "it would scandalise Mr. Li to a degree. Besides, we should be very uncomfortable. it is perfectly all right, I assure you. We have known Li for years. He is a great friend of ours. I assure you there is no occasion for uneasiness. He is just as civilised as we are."

Mr. Little looked perplexed.

"What do you think, Miss Morris?" he asked, turning to Stella.

Stella hesitated for a moment, knowing that the watching eyes of all the Chinese women were upon her, and that there was always a chance that one of the slave-girls might have picked up enough pidgin to follow what was being said.

"I think," she said at length, "that if Mr. Li means to be friendly, we are perfectly all right; and if he doesn't, there is nothing we can do."

"And do you think he means to be friendly?"

"I have no idea."

"Oh, Stella, darling, don't be so silly," chimed in Mrs. Hope. "Of course he means to be friendly. He is one of our oldest friends. Why should he have pressed us to stop if he didn't want us?"

"Why indeed?" thought Stella.

"Well, Mrs. Hope," said the old Quaker, "I am of Miss Morris's opinion—there is nothing we can do. We are completely in his hands. We can only trust in God and wait for the morning," and he entered his allotted room and shut the door behind him.

The rest of the party moved on. They came to another large and handsomely furnished room, containing twin beds. Into this Rosemary and Mrs. Hope were ushered. Mrs. Hope, who was very annoyed with Stella, ignored her and did not bid her good-night; Rosemary gave her cousin a wave of the hand and said:

"See you in the morning."

"I wonder," thought Stella to herself.

Then Stella went on alone. They went some considerable distance through the great rambling house of a Chinese grandee, and finally reached the part that had not been modernised, and Stella found herself shown into a purely Chinese room. The little handmaidens would have helped her undress in due form, but she sent them away. They went, protesting, closing the door behind them. There was a bolt on the door, but Stella did not trouble to fasten it, knowing the complete uselessness of such a precaution. For on the opposite side of the room a door leading into a garden stood wide open, and a glance had shown her there was no means of securing that.

She went across and stood on the sill gazing out into the small walled garden, all colourless in the moonlight, watching great moths at work collecting honey. It was an exquisite little *pleasaunce*, such as the Chinese love. And the room, too, was exquisite as a work of art; in fact every object in it was a work of art, and priceless. It was more like a museum than a bedroom. There was no electric light here, as in the rest of the house, and a Chinese lamp of ancient bronze burnt a scented oil upon a stand in its centre.

Stella went and sat on the edge of the great dragon-guarded bed, and waited. Somehow, now that there was only Li to be dealt with and no further need for concealment, she felt her nerve coming back to her.

Time went by, and nothing happened, and she was beginning to think she was following a false scent, when a shadow fell across the moonlit garden, and in another moment the tail figure of Li Wu Lu stood framed in the doorway.

"It is I, Yan Tai," he said. "Am I welcome?"

Stella did not answer for a moment, steadying herself as a horse is steadied for the jump, for she knew that all their lives, and something more than life for her, hung on her handling of Li in this crisis.

"My friend is always welcome," she said at length, her voice surprising even herself by its steadiness.

"I am not your friend, Yan Tai, I am your lover. Am I welcome?"

Stella paused again, and then she spoke, and in some strange way, with those pauses, the situation seemed to pass into her hands. It would not be Li who offered terms to her, but she who offered terms to Li.

So far as I know," she said, "there has never been any disgrace in my family. I come of a long line of honourable women, and it is not in my power to yield to you. There is a kind of steel backbone in me that just won't let me bend. I know what you said about the shop in the Gordon Road is common sense. But there it is—that steel spine—and all those honourable women—they just won't let me."

Li walked slowly across the room.

"May I sit down?" he said, seating himself at the foot of the dragon bed. "I won't do you any harm. I couldn't if I wanted to, I have been smoking too much opium."

"Oh, Wu Lu, don't do that," cried Stella in distress, quite forgetful of her peril at his hands. "You are too good a man to take to opium."

"One has to have something to take the edge off things, little star."

"I haven't had anything to take the edge off things. I've just had to stick it. And I've had my aunt battering at me as well."

"Then—if you feel like that about it, why won't you come to the house on the cliff as I suggested? You admit it is the common-sense solution."

"I have told you why—because of that spine of steel. It won't bend, Wu Lu. Common sense doesn't apply to it."

"Well, Yan Tai, you are killing me. I don't know if that means anything to you."

"It wouldn't work, Wu Lu. It wouldn't work, even if I came to the house on the cliff. I shouldn't be able to give you anything worth having. My heart wouldn't be in it. Everything I am would be just dried up. You would be no better off with me that you are with your concubines."

"No," said Li in an expressionless voice, "if you kept back your heart, I certainly shouldn't be. Not as well off, in fact, because you have not been trained."

There was silence between them, Li seeming sunk in thought. Stella could see that even in the short time he had been at it, the opium had taken its toll of him.

At length he spoke, still in the same monotonous voice without any expression in it.

"If I had known that any woman had the power to make me suffer SO much, I would have killed you, Yan Tai, as soon as I found you were getting such a hold over me."

Stella put out her hand and took his as it rested on the silk coverlet beside her. She felt something hard in the palm, and raising the limp, unresponsive hand, she drew out from the loose silk sleeve the long slender stiletto of the Chinese assassin.

"Yes, I came to kill you," said Li, letting her take it unresistingly.

Stella laid the foot-long blade, like a miniature rapier, on the coverlet between them.

"You can kill me if you want to, Wu Lu," she said. "It might be the simplest solution for both of us"

He did not answer.

She took his hand again. He paid no attention whatever, sitting beside her with averted face as if hypnotised.

"Wu Lu," she said, "we are both desperately unhappy. We have got to help each other."

"Will you come to the house on the cliff, Yan Tai?" he repeated in the same expressionless voice.

"No, it wouldn't work. My heart wouldn't be in it."

"Perhaps you are right," he said. "It wouldn't work."

She felt the hand that she held suddenly tense itself, and knew that he was getting ready to snatch up the knife and plunge it in her breast.

She spoke again, commanding the situation and the man by her very quietness.

"No, Wu Lu, I will not come to the house on the cliff, but I tell you what I will do—I will face the difficulties of a mixed marriage if you will."

She heard Li give a gasp, and the hand she held suddenly gripped hers rigidly.

"No, Stella," he said in a broken voice, "I have told you I cannot do that. My influence is the only thing that stands between my country and anarchy. If we can maintain order, we can save South China, and may even be able to reconquer North China in time. Shall I throw away my country for the sake of a woman? I cannot do it."

"Then you had better kill and be done with it," said Stella.

He sat silently for a while, but whether in thought or in apathy, she could not tell.

Finally Stella broke the silence that seemed to be going on indefinitely.

"Something has got to be done about you, Wu Lu. I cannot stand by and see you knocking yourself to pieces over me like this. I would be willing to live in retirement like a Chinese wife, if that would be any help to you."

Li roused himself.

"Yes, Stella, it would be a very great help," he said, his voice sounding more natural than it had done since the dreadful interview started.

Then he fell silent again, but it was a more natural silence, and she saw he was working things out in his mind, trying to see how they could be done. Finally he spoke.

"I do not mind the odium of a mixed marriage. It will be nothing new to me, I have been an outcast all my life. Outcast from the whites because of my colour. Outcast from my own people because I will not observe custom. The only thing that troubles me is that I am pretty certain the patriots will turn against me if I make a mixed marriage because they will say I have betrayed the spirit of China. I am the only person who can hold things together, because I hold the Tongs; and if we split our party, everything will break up in every direction. As long as I hold things together down here, we have got a nucleus from which we can rebuild; but if I let go, I let anarchy loose. it is a terrible thing to let anarchy loose; if you had seen some of the devastated provinces, you would know how terrible it is."

Stella sat rigid. Was a woman's honour worth this price?

She spoke in a muffled voice.

"I will come to the house on the cliff if you want me to, Wu Lu."

"No, Stella," he replied quietly, "I don't want you to. You were quite right, it wouldn't work. What I want with you—what you have to give me, if you will give it—wouldn't be found in the house on the cliff. We must face this thing and see it straight through without subterfuge. The feeling I have for you goes too deep for makeshifts. But you see my difficulty, don't you? I would despise myself, and probably hate you, if I betrayed my country for a woman. It has been done so often, and it is so—cheap."

They sat silent again, hand in hand, and Stella realised as never before the amazing, purposeless cruelty of race prejudice. There was not a single thing to be said for it, so far as she could see. It sprang from the most primitive, least rational impulses in human nature; decent people with any intelligence invariably rose above it individually; but in the mass it justified callousness beyond belief.

She looked at Li as he sat beside her. He seemed ominously quiet. Then suddenly he spoke.

"How old are you, Stella?"

"Nineteen."

"I thought you were. That was a very good offer you made me—Yan Tai."

"What do you mean?"

"If you are only nineteen, you cannot marry me without your family's permission, and when I go to ask their permission, after letting you all get out of here with whole skins, what do you suppose they will say to me? Yes, that was a very good offer indeed, my star."

He suddenly whipped round like a striking snake; Stella felt a grip of steel on her shoulder, thrusting her down among the cushions, and the long blade of the knife was at her throat. She looked up into a face like a devil-mask.

Some instinct warned her to lie still. If she struggled, she knew that knife would instantly be thrust home. Nerve, and more nerve, was her only chance. She looked straight back into eyes that were not eyes at all, but just black slits.

"Kill if you want to, Wu Lu," she said, "but don't kill for that reason, for it isn't true. I never thought of that when I spoke."

He continued to stare at her for a long minute, his face set in its terrible expression as if cast in yellow metal. Then the hand that held the knife drew back to his ear and shot forward like a spring released; the knife flew across the room and plunged into

141

the panel of a lacquer cabinet and stuck there quivering.

"I am sorry, Yan Tai," said he, releasing her. "I believe you. I think you speak the truth."

Stella sat up and mechanically pushed back the tortoise shell pins into the loosened coils of silky black hair at the nape of her neck.

"I think you are mad," she said. "Is it going to be like this if I marry you?"

"No, I'd be all right then. Stella, do you realise what my life has been like, cut off from both races? People say Eurasians are rotten because of their mixed blood, but it isn't that, it's because of the conditions they live under. I know, and I'm pure-bred if any one ever was; but I've got a Eurasian mentality, all the same. And I know why so many Jews are anarchists, too. I'd use dynamite myself, only I've no need to. I've got money, and it's a much more effective explosive. Oh, Yan Tai, it is a rotten business, this race problem; it's poisoned the very roots of life for me. It doesn't give you a chance."

"But Wu Lu, everybody speaks awfully highly of you. You're tremendously respected, you are really."

"You bet I am, Stella, I've got a stranglehold on every one of them through my bank. They can't turn over in bed without my permission. I've spent ten years getting it, and I've got it—but a stranglehold does not give you comradeship. I made them elect me to their club. I'm the only yellow man that ever has been elected to one of those clubs—and when I come into the room, conversation stops or becomes formal. It isn't a club when I'm in it."

"But don't your own people stick to you?"

"Stick to me? No, Stella. They'd stick a knife in me if they dared because they say I play into the hands of the whites. They call me the foreign devil in the yellow skin. Oh, it's a lovely mix-up! If we married, we couldn't have any children. I'd never let a child go through what I've been through. Why can't you people leave us alone or make up your minds to accept us? If you educate a man, accept him as an educated man, don't kick him back where he no longer belongs. It's hell for him, and he

142

raises hell for you. That's what's losing you India. Why can't you take a man for what he is—ignorant or educated, straight or crooked? But you people seem to think that the worst white man is better than the best coloured man. I wish you could have seen your white face when you saw my yellow one! If I'd had a grain of sense, I'd never have looked at you again. But you went and smiled at me, you little wretch, and finished me off completely. A man who is emotionally starved is so abominably vulnerable."

"Wu Lu, I didn't turn against you when I saw you were Chinese. I was taken by surprise, that was all. If you want to know the truth, I was attracted. I was horribly hurt when you cut me dead; I was quite prepared to be friendly."

"I wasn't. I knew perfectly well the sort of hell I was brewing for myself. When I saw you under the gas lamp at the station you took my breath away, you were so beautiful."

"That simply amazes me. I have always thought of myself as quite the Plain Jane."

"You are not. Not to any one except Anglo-Saxons, anyway. The French and the Russians are raving about you. If you were not dotless, your uncle would have been inundated with proposals for your hand. As for the Chinese— Never you take chances with a Chinese, Stella. Nobody would rape Rosemary except to annoy her; she is safe as houses. But with you, it is a different matter."

"And I had always thought I was so safe because I was not attractive."

"Stella, you are the most beautiful thing I have ever seen. The most beautiful the sweetest the best. It is not a case of attraction. It goes much deeper than that. If it had just been attraction I should have got over it during the three months I was away from you. That was why I went away—to try and get over it. But I didn't get over it. I'll never get over it. We'll live together or die together, Stella. Yes, I'll marry you if you want me to. I don't care. Let my people go hang."

"But, Wu Lu, if you marry me in that spirit no good can come of it."

143

"No good can come of it anyway, Yan Tai."

Stella looked at him.

"My word, you've gone to pieces properly," she said.

"Yes, haven't I? What did you expect? I suppose you thought I'd got Anglo-Saxon stamina. Well, I haven't. I've got ten times your depth of feeling instead. And then my white training comes in—I can't even kill you; I haven't the heart. Stella, listen—your battery's in the little temple in the terrace. Go and put it in the car; you know how, don't you ?—and get your people out. Wake them up and get them out."

"And what are you going to do with yourself after we're gone?"

"Never mind that. Go while the going's good."

"I do mind, though. I mind ever so much, Wu Lu. I mind just as much as you do. Look here, I've got Anglo-Saxon stamina if you haven't. We're going through with this. You're going to marry me, Wu Lu, and I'm going to make you happy. And you're going to tell your people that your private life is none of their business, and if they don't want you to work for them politically any longer, that's their look-out. And I'm going to tell my people to go to blazes. They won't want much telling—they haven't far to go. And we'll have a jolly good shot at making a success of the thing, and if we go down, we'll go down fighting; but we won't go down without a jolly good try at it."

Li lifted his head from his hands and looked at her.

"Hein," he said. "Mother of Empire-builders!"

"Well, will you take it on?"

"My star, when you look at me like that, you can do anything you like with me. There is only one thing you must not do!"

'What is that?"

"Let me down once YOU have taken me on."

"I won't let YOU down, Wu Lu."

"No, I know you won't, I am content"

"Tell me one thing, had YOU planned to kidnap me?"

"Yes. I'd have had you if You'd gone up the Pass, but YOU turned too soon."

"What would you have done with me if You'd caught me?"

"Don't ask, Yan Tai, I was mad. Let us forget it. That reminds me, though, I've caught somebody, and I the haven't vaguest idea who it is. Some one who came along in the car after you. I suppose I'll have that to straighten out to-morrow."

"To-morrow?" said Stella. "To-day, you mean. It's been to-morrow for some time. Go to bed, Wu Lu, we're as sleepy as two owls."

He rose obediently. "I see my domestic bondage is beginning."

He stood looking down at her as she lay curled up among the crumpled cushions. Then he took her face between his hands.

"I suppose you will expect me to kiss you, but I am not very good at kissing. It has never appealed to me. Bless you, my star. You are the most beautiful thing I have ever seen. You have made me very, very happy because you think of me just as a man—not a yellow man, or a rich man, or even, perhaps, as a man at all—but just as a some one like yourself, with feelings that can be hurt. And I think you like to see me happy, Yan Tai, and hate hurting me. It is so different from everything I have been accustomed to. And I trust you as I have never trusted any other living being. And do you know why I trust you, little star?"

"No, why do you trust me?"

"Because I know that you are not afraid of me."

"Are people generally afraid of you, Wu Lu?"

"Yes, Stella, I always make them afraid of me because it is the only hold I have over them. But I know I couldn't make you afraid of me, whatever I did to you. 'Kill and be done with it,' is all you would say to me, and I love you for it. I have never seen anything like you, Stella-—half boy, half girl—half child, half woman—I shall be the most envied man east of Suez. You were quite right, the house on the cliff was a stupid idea."

CHAPTER XII

STELLA dropped back on the cushions as physically exhausted as if she had taken part in a struggle. The crisis had come and gone, she hardly knew how. She only knew that she was going to marry Li Wu Lu, and that although she loved him, she felt more as if she had been sentenced to death than affianced, She wondered how she would get through the awful interregnum between the announcement of the engagement and the marriage. Li, she knew, had enormous resources and was as clever as the Devil, but she did not see how in the world he could protect her from the wrath of her family as long as she was in their hands.

And after she had passed into his hands? Somehow that did not worry her so much. She was so surprised to find herself alive at all that just to be alive seemed all that was needful. She felt fairly certain that Li would not be unkind to her unless she crossed him, but of what he was capable when crossed she had already seen a pretty representative sample. She could not help being amused at Li's standard of ethics, so totally at variance with his vaunted European mentality.

Well, there was only one thing she could do—take him as she found him; she couldn't alter him, that was quite certain. And something within her was glad that she had followed her heart and not played for safety. There was suffering ahead of her, she knew that, there might even be death, but she would know the big things that come to a woman, and she was glad Wu Lu was happy. It did not seem to matter very much what became of her; she had been terribly worried at seeing him go all to pieces, but now that he was all right there did not seem anything left to worry about.

As he had truly divined, the distress of another distressed her; his colour or class made no difference, she felt for the pain; the fact that a yellow man ought not to fall in love with a white girl did not count. She quite realised that it would have been better if it had never happened, but it had happened, and something had got to be done about it.

She had done the only thing she could think of—unless she were willing to leave him to break up until there was no more left of him.

Deep inside she was satisfied with what she had done, even if her marriage to Li ended as mixed marriages are always supposed to end. It might. She didn't know, she had no experience of the world; all the same, she did not see why it should. She was satisfied that if it did go on the rocks, it would not be because of anything Li Wu Lu might do, but because they would be unable to withstand the pressure that would be brought to bear on them, and she felt that she would sooner go down with the man she had come to love than save herself at his expense; that Li would go down if she did not stand by him, she felt pretty certain.

Her decision taken, she was at peace; the struggle would begin again when her family learnt what was before them; until then, she could enjoy her secret happiness unmolested. The storm would break in due course, but its time was not yet. She lay back on the soft silken cushions relaxed, enjoying the peace and freedom. She had meant to get up, and get undressed, and put on the exquisite Chinese sleeping-robe that lay on a stool beside her, but instead she dropped off, just as she was, into the dead sleep of exhaustion among the cushions.

When she awoke it was broad daylight. What the time might be, she did not know, for needless to say, she had forgotten to wind her watch. At the first creak of a board under her foot as she stepped off the bed, in shot the beaming little handmaidens, who had evidently been sitting on the threshold. She wondered how long they had been waiting there. They would have thought nothing of sitting there all night, and Li would have thought nothing of it, either.

They whipped her out of her crumpled clothes, and popped her into a bath-tub, and poured warm scented water all over her, and by the time they had got her out and dried and massaged, her undies were back, freshly washed and ironed. Then, by the time they had fixed her face and done her hair, her frock reappeared also, looking as if it had come straight from Bond Street. But they did not give her back her bead necklet, but with many giggles put round her neck what she thought must be pearls, though they were like no pearls she had ever seen, being a pale shadowy pink.

She did not dare refuse them for fear of hurting Li's feelings, but she thought with a shudder of the barrage of questions and comments she would have to endure as soon as her family noticed them. Luckily, however, the necklet was a long one, and slipped down inside the folds of her cross-over bodice discreetly.

Meanwhile in other rooms other scenes were being enacted. Rosemary, wearing Li's pyjamas, which were much too tight for her, sat up in her very comfortable bed and yawned and stretched herself.

"I say, Mummie, do you think Li means to hold us to ransom?" she said.

"My dear child, don't be so ridiculous. He wouldn't dare. And besides, he's one of our oldest friends. Surely you know that."

"I know we've known him ever since he was a lanky youth and I was a sprat, but I have never been able to under stand why you think he's such a great friend. Personally, I should have said he hated us."

"Don't be so ridiculous, Rosemary. If he hates us, why does he see so much of us? "

"Perhaps he believes in keeping an eye on us. This 'put you up for the night' business smells fishy to me. It's rather a lark, all the same. I think I'd rather enjoy being kidnapped by Li, provided he feeds us on the same scale as he did last night."

In the other guest-room Mrs. Little had commended herself to God and gone to sleep, but Mr. Little had sat up all night.

At dawn they had arisen—they had not undressed — and were now, with true Quaker philosophy, awaiting the summons to breakfast or execution as the case might be.

"What do you make of the situation, William," asked Mrs. Little of her husband. "There seems to me to be some thing very queer afoot. That poor child was frightened to death. She knows something her aunt doesn't. It looks to me as if that Chinaman had some sort of hold over her. She was real scared of him, and he knew it."

"I don't know what to think, Minnie. Li's reputation stands very high commercially, and it is unlikely that he would do anything to get himself into trouble with either their country or ours. He will not want two consuls in pursuit of him simultaneously. The Hopes are influential people, and George would pull strings on our behalf. Personally, I think we are safe enough, but I am not at all happy about that little girl. It looks to me as if she had got herself involved with native life and was in serious difficulties."

"I think she's got herself involved with Li," said Mrs. Little. "I guess we have sat up here quite long enough. I suggest we walk about the house and see what is happening."

She opened the door, and two bowing little handmaidens awaited them on the threshold, one of whom, in quite good English, invited them to descend to where breakfast awaited them on the terrace. There was nothing else to be done, so they followed the handmaidens out into the garden. There they found a table laid for six, English fashion.

"We're all expected to be alive, anyway," said Mrs. Little with a sigh of relief as she counted the plates.

From the far end of the terrace they saw a man in a white suit advancing towards them.

"Who is this?" said Mr. Little, "and what is he doing here?"

Mrs. Little breathed a prayer of thanks to Heaven; but as the man drew nearer, she withdrew it again, for they saw that the wearer of the European clothes was a Chinese. But it was not until he spoke to them that they realised it was Li, for he looked so completely and utterly different from what he had done the previous night. It was not merely that the European clothes changed his appearance, as they would that of any man, but the man himself seemed completely different.

He was in very high spirits, that was plain; and he didn't look as if he had anything on his conscience, either. But then you could never tell with the Chinese, they had such queer consciences.

He behaved as any English or American host would have behaved, enquiring after their health and comfort with conventional solicitude; in fact, as Mrs. Hope had said, you would never have known he was Chinese if it hadn't been for his face.

"I think our friends will soon be with us," he told them, "I have heard their bath-water."

That sounded very reassuring. People who have been murdered do not wash.

Then Stella appeared at the end of the terrace, accompanied by the rapturous Tsi, who got under her feet so often that in self-defence she picked him up. Li greeted her in Chinese, and she answered in the same language, but she was so busy dodging Tsi's pink tongue and extreme affection that it was difficult to judge what might be her state of mind. Then Mrs. Hope and Rosemary came in sight, and the usual clatter of conversation began that always enveloped Mrs. Hope. Li was immensely affable to them also. In fact, the only person he had greeted without gush was Stella.

Then they sat down and ate an English breakfast. Mrs. Little, who was watching Stella with a motherly eye, noted that she looked considerably better than she had done the previous evening, but there was still something very tense and mask-like about her face.

"You will be glad to hear that your battery has been recovered," Li informed the company. " A little boy, the son of my gardener, he took it for his motor-cycle. He has been beaten and the battery has been put back."

Mrs. Hope expressed satisfaction. Stella appeared to be having difficulty in keeping a straight face.

After breakfast Li announced that he must go into the Concession himself this morning, and as his car had not yet come back, he asked if they would give him a lift. Mrs. Hope, only too proud to show off the very old friend of the family to all and sundry, readily agreed, and he was crammed in between Stella and Mr. Little.

Li, half sideways to economise room, laid his arm along the back of the seat behind Stella's shoulders. This was not lost upon the observers in the back seat.

"Look at Li, he'd cuddle Stella for two twos," commented Rosemary. "Dashed if I'd have a Chink all over me like that." Being an expert and persistent necker herself, she was very critical of anybody else's exploits within the prohibited degrees of relationship. "You ought to tread on it, Mummie, Esperanza House will get sniffed at if we let this sort of thing go on. If you say it's quite all right because he's one of our oldest friends, I shall bite your ear."

"I shall certainly speak to Stella when we get back. She's a great deal too free with Li; it's not wise with a Chinaman."

"It would be much more to the point if you spoke to Li. It's him that's doing it, not her."

"I don't want unpleasantness with Li because of your father, Rosemary, he's a—"

"Oh, gawks, don't say that again!"

Meanwhile the object of their condemnation, evidently feeling very much at his ease despite the crush, took off his hat and pushed it into the parcel-net in the roof of the car, revealing to the watchers the back of a head that looked exactly like black lacquer.

"Makes himself at home, doesn't he?" said Rosemary.

"Well, dear, he's one of our—"

"Oh, Mummy, shut up!"

"If you can afford to quarrel with Li, your father can't," snapped Mrs. Hope.

"So we've got to put up with his amorous advances in order that Pa can coin cash? I call it no better than common prostitution," said Rosemary, who, being a modern young miss, had the vocabulary of a bargee.

"Rosemary, be quiet!" hissed Mrs. Hope, suddenly realising that they were shouting at each other as their habit was, and their voices might carry above the noise of the car; they would certainly reach Mrs. Little's ears, anyway.

That voices could carry even above the racket of the family bus was evidenced by the fact that they could hear Li and Stella wrangling amicably with each other, and giving proof of the assertion that he was a very great friend of a part of the family, anyway.

"Hein, Stella, you will see a devastated province for yourself if you drive like that," cried Li, snatching on the handbrake as they came round a bend and saw a family party ahead of them. Being a fast driver himself, he was nervous as a cat of any one else's fast driving.

"Put your hands in your pockets, Wu Lu, and keep them there; I won't have my driving interfered with while I'm at the wheel."

"And I won't have my chances of survival interfered with. Slow up to twenty, or I'll keep the hand-brake on all the time and make you run in second."

"Twenty be hanged, this isn't a funeral."

"It will be, if you drive any faster than twenty on this road."

To emphasise the truth of his words, they came round a hairpin bend and found the sea beneath their front wheels.

"Ooo-er—!" said Stella, backing the car cautiously.

"My star, I have had enough of this; you are going to let me drive, for I know the road, and you don't."

Stella was not averse, for she had scared herself by this last miscalculation; moreover she knew that with Li slamming on the hand-brake as the fancy took him, they had the makings of a skid on the leaf-strewn road, especially if he elected to brake when she elected to jump clear by accelerating.

"All right," she said, "but you'll both have to get out before I can move, because this door is out of commission."

"No need; you stand up, and I'll slide in behind you, and

then you can drop into my place."

Stella stood up as bid. It was a manoeuvre commonly done in such a roomy car as the old Daimler. But Mrs. Hope wasn't having any. That sort of crawling over each other might do with Rosemary's young men, but it wasn't going to be done with Asiatics.

"Please don't do that," she said in icy tones. "It would be much better if Mr. Little would be good enough to get out and let you change over properly. Sit down, please, Stella."

Stella sat down as bid; but unfortunately Li had already accomplished his half of the change-over, and she sat on his knee.

"Hein," said Li, "there was no need to trouble Mr. Little; still, if you prefer it that way, we will wait for him."

Stella, her cheeks burning, shoved at the pair of them indiscriminately till she was able to force herself down between them. Li grunted as her elbow took him in the ribs.

"Hein, my star," he said, moving over as far as he could to make room for her. "It is fortunate it is you and not your cousin." Which remark, being overheard in the back seat, did not add to the peace of families.

Then he took over the driving, but what with Stella's propinquity and the unfamiliar car on the difficult road, he was not making a very good job of it either. Moreover, he had a tendency to gesticulate when he talked. They came round a corner into a funeral procession, dodged the corpse by a hair's breadth, and chased the mourners all over the road.

"Mind what you're doing, Wu Lu!" cried Stella. You're qualifying for a job on the trams!"

As the driving of the trams was notorious for its badness, this was a dire insult.

"You're qualifying for an inside seat in that vehicle we've just passed if you cheek me any more, Miss Star."

"Real chummy, aren't they?" said Rosemary *sotto voce*. "Why does she call him Wu Lu? Is that his Christian name?"

Fortunately for all concerned, they arrived at the boundary of the Concession at that moment, and the officer of the guard on the gate came running out at the sight of them.

"My God, Mrs. Hope, we're glad to see you!" " he exclaimed as they pulled up for the inspection. "Where have you been?"

"We had engine trouble and couldn't start up again after stopping for tea at Pei-Chi, and Mr. Li very kindly put us up for the night and sent a messenger in to tell my husband."

"The messenger never arrived. We've been in a blue funk about you. There's been another party gone astray on the road you were following, and it's pretty certain they've been kidnapped. Well, I'm dashed glad to see you safe and sound. I'll phone up your house and let them know to expect you. Your husband has been carrying on like all possessed."

They drove on, and in a few minutes were at the door of Esperanza House.

"May I come in a moment, Mrs. Hope ?" said Li. "I want to have a word with your husband, and I expect I can catch him here."

Mrs. Hope gave a rather chilly permission. She daren't be too cordial to Li after the way he had been behaving, because Rosemary, who had more than her fair share of colour prejudice, would have given her such a wigging.

"Won't you have lunch with us?" she added. It was hardly advisable suddenly to cool off towards the very old friend of the family, especially with the new lease of the Hope Navigation Co.'s premises still unsigned.

"Thank you, I should like to, but may I leave it undecided for the moment? Maybe I shall have to go straight on down to the bank after I have seen your husband."

Stella felt her heart miss a beat, and an icy cold feeling went all down her back. She thought she knew what he wanted to see her uncle about.

Mr. Hope appeared on the steps, embraced his wife and daughter warmly, and gave Stella a perfunctory peck. Mrs. Hope told their story in her addle-pated way, and Mr. Hope, who never expected to make head or tail of any story as told by her, listened to all she had to say, and seeing that they seemed to be quite all right, thanked Li warmly for his hospitality without troubling himself overmuch with the discrepancies.

Li repeated his request for an interview, and they went off together to the study while the rest of the party went into the inner lounge hall. There they found the tame cat, who had already got the cocktail cabinet open and was having one, to the horror of Mrs. Hope, who had carefully camouflaged that cabinet with a bowl of flowers.

"So here you are, safe and sound? There's been the dickens of a confuffle about you," he greeted them. "I hear Li put you all up for the night. How in the world did you come across him?

"We happened to be passing Pei-Chi, so we looked in."

"My goodness, you've got a nerve. Didn't you know he'd been on the bust? He was due for a magnificent hang over, if for nothing worse."

"Oh, I don't believe that sort of gossip. I speak no evil, no, nor listen to it. He was very charming to us, anyway; you see, he's a—" she caught Rosemary's eye and shut up hastily.

But something had caught the connoisseur's eye. He put out his hand to Stella's breast and lifted the pearl necklace from among the loose folds of her frock and looked at it intently.

"You are a very fortunate young woman," he said, "but I shouldn't wear this when you go motoring if I were you. It may get you murdered."

"What, Stella murdered for her pink beads?" jeered Rosemary.

"Rosemary, your eye is as uncultivated as your mind. By the way, Miss Stella, I suppose you realise the value of your 'pink beads'?"

"I do not know exactly what they are worth, but I know they must be valuable."

"They certainly are—very valuable. You need never lack money as long as you have these—only don't leave them about in a cardboard box on your dressing-table."

It was now Mrs. Hope's turn to examine Stella's necklace.

But what kind of stone are they—Stella's pink beads? I thought she had got them at Woolworth's, and that they were

155

not in the best of taste. You know their long strings of mock pearls—sixpence a foot. Quite pretty as long as they are small, but those are too large."

"Don't you know pearls when you see them, Florence?"

"But these are pink."

"Have you never heard of pink pearls?"

"No, never. What a funny idea. Pink pearls—it seems a contradiction in terms."

"You do not often see them in England, where complexions are fair, but they are much prized on the Continent because they are more becoming to brunettes than the white ones. I don't know what your necklace would fetch in Paris or Rome, Miss Stella, but it would be a pretty handsome figure. It is not only the quality of those pearls, but the matching that is so amazing. It must have taken an expert a lifetime to collect that necklace."

"How did you come by that necklace, Stella?" asked Mrs. Hope.

"It was given me."

"Who gave it you?"

"That is my business."

"Don't be impudent. Answer my question. Who gave it you?"

"I shouldn't press that question, if I were you," said Mr. Mathers in a low voice.

Mrs. Hope cast a contemptuous look at Stella.

"If I had known you had that necklace to fall back on," she said, "I should not have bothered to ask you out here." .

Mr. Mathers hastily changed the subject. "Did you hear that the Anstruthers have been kidnapped up on the neck of the pass? Exactly the spot where you were to have gone if Stella hadn't missed the turning."

"Yes, so they were telling us at the gate."

"Stella's bad driving spared us something, anyway," said Rosemary, who was not ill-natured, and got rather fed up with the constant nagging of her cousin.

But her well-meant intervention was ill-timed, for it reminded Mrs. Hope of her grievances against Stella, and that her niece needed speaking to.

"If you ever drive again as you did yesterday, Stella, it's the last time you go out in the car."

This was not a very terrible threat, as Stella was sick to death of pottering about in the badly-running car, a straight forward trip being the exception among a lot of taxying.

"I hope you realise how very stupid your behaviour was— upsetting everything and making everybody nervous with your silly imaginings; and here we are—back again perfectly safely after all."

"I'm glad you're satisfied," said Stella.

Suddenly, from the study, they heard pandemonium break out. Mr. Hope was shouting at the top of his voice, in a towering rage.

"Good God," exclaimed Mrs. Hope, forgetting that the Littles must not be sworn in front of. "What in the world's happening?"

They heard footsteps cross the outer hail, and the slam of the front door. Then heavier footsteps followed, and Mr. Hope appeared through the curtains, his face scarlet with rage.

"Well, here's a pretty kettle of fish!" " he exclaimed.

"My God, Florence, what in the world possessed you to go to Li's house?"

"We've often been to Li's house. Why shouldn't I go?"

"You knew there was trouble afoot, why didn't you keep clear?"

"Why—why—what's the matter?" quavered Mrs. Hope, wondering what she had put her foot into now.

"What's the matter? The matter is that Li wants to marry Stella."

"Good God! But he can't, she's under age."

"That's what I told him. And he had the cheek to ask for our permission."

"Did you give it?"

"What do you take me for? Of course I didn't."

"That settles it, then," said Mrs. Hope with a sigh of relief.

"It settles that point all right, but it means I've made an enemy for life of Li."

"Does that matter so very much?"

"Yes, it does matter, very much indeed. It's damned awkward."

He turned savagely to Stella. " So this is what we get for providing for you and showing you kindness."

"I admit you provided for me," said Stella; "but I never noticed any kindness."

"Don't bandy words with me. You're going home by the next boat."

"Yes," chimed in Mrs. Hope, "and you'll go home at your own expense, too. I don't see why we should pay your expenses again. You can sell that pearl necklace of yours, which you were given 'for services rendered,' I suppose."

"What's this about a pearl necklace," demanded Mr. Hope.

His wife pointed to it silently. He stared.

"Good God, how did you come by that, Stella? Li give it you?"

Stella hesitated a moment, and then said: "Yes."

There was a dead silence.

"When?"

"This morning."

"For—'services rendered'?"

"No, as an engagement present."

"Do you expect us to believe that?"

"No."

"I believe it, Stella," said Mrs. Little quietly.

Mr. Hope swung round on her angrily, then remembered who she was, and thought better of it.

"We won't discuss the matter any further now. It's settled, and that's the end of it. Stella goes back by the next boat. It's the one she came out on, so she may encounter a few tales there, which won't do her any harm—to see how conduct like hers is regarded by decent people. Now we'll go and have lunch and get the taste of this business out of our mouths."

They all trooped into the dining-room, including the tame

cat, to whom Stella was very grateful, for he took charge of the conversation and kept it going.

She was not unduly worried. Her uncle might storm and bluster, but Li had enormous resources at his disposal, both direct and indirect, and was reputed to be as clever as the devil, and she felt that she only had to keep quiet, and put up with temporary unpleasantness, and everything would come right. She was very happy about what she chose to regard as her engagement, in spite of the refusal of her legal guardians to ratify it. She had done the thing her heart demanded, and was prepared to damn the consequences at the present moment. She knew that Li was happy and at peace, and that made her still happier.

As they were finishing lunch one of the boys came in with a note on a salver, which he proceeded to deliver to her.

"Bring that to me," said Mr. Hope before she could pick it up, and the boy obediently went round to the head of the table, but not before Stella had seen the words: 'If undelivered, return to the Inland and Overseas Commercial Bank,' printed across the top of the envelope.

Mr. Hope tore it open, but irregular festoons of Chinese characters met his eyes.

"I will take this down to the office and get it translated," he said.

"That letter is for me, not for you," said Stella. "You have no right to touch it."

"You are under age, and your aunt and I are your legal guardians, and a pretty pickle you've let us in for. There's going to be no nonsense about letters, or telephone calls, or anything else, believe me."

"I can't see why you bother. You could get me off your hands this way and be rid of me."

"And what about the scandal? We mind that if you don't. Do you suppose I want a houseful of yellow relatives in the very town? And what about Rosemary? What chance has she of making a decent marriage if you go and make a dirty mess in this very house? No, there will be no mixed marriages in this family."

Stella went to her room and flung herself exhausted on her bed. She was furious that Li's letter—her first love letter—should have been seen by any eyes but her own; she wondered what he would have to say about it when he heard, and whether he would live up to his reputation for vengefulness.

A tap at the door roused her, and with a sigh she flung on a faded old negligee of Rosemary's and went to open it. There she found Mrs. Little. Stella did not want to talk about her affairs, they were too sore, and sympathy was too unlikely, and she admitted her reluctantly.

"My dear, I am afraid you have been having a very troubled time, and a very troubled time is ahead of you."

Stella acquiesced apathetically.

"Mr. Little and I were wondering if you would like to come with us up country for a little trip; it would help you to put things behind you."

"It is awfully kind of you, but I have no intention of putting things behind me; I am going through with them."

"Are you really, my dear? Tell me frankly, what is your motive?"

"Partly because I am honour bound, and partly because I really want to."

"Are you—fond of this Mr. Li, my dear?"

"Yes."

"Then, in that case, I respect you for going through with it. We had thought—I do not quite know what we had thought, but we did not think that you cared for him."

"Well, you are wrong, I do."

"Well, my dear, it is a difficult problem. I admire your courage. He is a very fine man, and if any one could make a success of a mixed marriage, he could; but it is difficult, very difficult. Still, it is not impossible if you are both wise and brave and really fond of each other. All the same, you are so young. I wish it could have been otherwise for you, Stella; you have difficulties ahead that you hardly realise."

"If there is anything worse than yesterday, I shall be very

much surprised."

"Why didn't you want to go to his house, dear? Hadn't you come to an understanding with him?"

"Far from it. We'd had a most fearful shindy and I'd put an end to everything. That was what they call his binge was about. It wasn't a binge at all; he had just gone all to pieces."

"Why didn't you tell your aunt this? She would never have insisted on going to Pei-Chi if she had known."

"Aunt Florence isn't the sort of person one tells things to. I might have said something if she'd been decent, but she rubbed it in about my being dependent on her charity, and I got fed up—I've had so much nagging that I just didn't care. I suppose you know you had a jolly narrow escape from being murdered?

"Is — this — the price you have had to pay to get us off?"

"Yes, it got you off, nothing else would have done. But that wasn't the only reason I did it. I'm really fond of him, you know."

"Well, my dear, I'm glad, and I'm sorry. Feeling as you both do about each other, I suppose you will be less unhappy if you go through with it than if you end it, especially as you have no prospects; but it is one of those things that ought never to have started."

"It got started in a fog. I didn't realise he was a Chinese until it was well under way; I just thought of him as a man I liked awfully, and once I'd got into the way of thinking of him as a man I liked, I couldn't suddenly turn round and think of him as Chinese. It just wouldn't work. I couldn't help liking him, and I hated hurting his feelings."

"Well," said the little Quakeress with a sigh, "I guess if we were never allowed to see people's colour till we had got to know them, there would be a lot less colour prejudice. I will say good-bye to you now, dear, if you won't come with us on our trip into the interior tomorrow, for we shall go to a hotel when we come back. All this quarrelling upsets Mr. Little terribly; he's had such indigestion since he's been in this house. I've never seen him so bad, and it isn't the cooking either."

"The servants call this place the House Where the Rice is Bitter."

"Well, I don't blame them. I think it just describes it."

But the assaults on Mr. Little's digestion were not yet over. When they arrived in the lounge for coffee, Mr. Hope threw an envelope across to Stella.

"There is your letter," he said. "Now I hope this will be the end of all this nonsense and it will never be referred to again. I suppose there is no need to tell you that in your own interests you had better keep your mouth shut, and I am going to ask Mr. and Mrs. Little to do likewise."

"Certainly," said Mr. Little. "We should have done that in any case."

Stella picked up her letter and placed it inside her frock.

"Read it and be done with it, Stella," said her uncle. This is a matter which concerns all of us, not just you."

Stella took out her letter with shaking hands and opened it. The translation, on the Hope Navigation Co.'s paper, was pinned to the original. She read it, being too far gone to wrestle with the Chinese characters. It was brief and to the point, and rendered in the commercial English of the compradore, it was extraordinarily shattering. Owing to circumstances over Which he had no control, Li could not go through with the marriage. He regretted any distress his conduct might have caused her, but was sure on mature consideration she would realise that it was the only possible course open to them, for, when all its consequences were considered, it was obvious that a mixed marriage was out of the question for both of them.

"I would like Mr. and Mrs. Little to see this, too," said Mr. Hope, "as they have been rather involved in the matter," and he took the letter out of Stella's unresisting hand and passed it over to the Quakers.

"Have we your permission, Miss Stella?" " said the old man. She nodded miserably. They read it. Mrs. Little's eyes met hers, and they handed it back without comment.

"The offer of a trip up country still holds good, my dear," said Mr. Little.

"What's that?" exclaimed Mr. Hope sharply, "have you been offering her a trip up country?"

"That is so," said the Quaker equably. "But she declined it in view of her forthcoming marriage."

"I take it in very bad part that you should do that without consulting us," said Mr. Hope, with a degree of agitation that caused them all to stare at him. "I certainly should not have agreed. She is going back to England by the next boat. It is the only thing to do with her in view of the way she behaves. We cannot possibly take the responsibility of her."

He turned to Stella again.

"That necklace must go back to Li, Stella. You can't keep it. Every one would know who gave it you, and why it was given."

"Yes, of course it must go back under the circumstances," said Stella wearily, "I wouldn't wish to keep it."

"Will you see about it, Florence?" he turned to his wife.

Stella took off the string of pearls and handed it to her aunt.

"Aren't they perfectly lovely!" exclaimed Mrs. Hope, running the globes of rosy light through her hands, quite forgetful of her condemnation of them as common when she had thought they came from Woolworth's.

"Do let me look," said Rosemary. "I have never had a close-up of really first-class pearls before. Aren't they simply gorgeous ! The shimmer seems to come from right inside them, not just off the surface. I shall never mistake imitations for real ones again now I've seen these. What do you suppose they're worth? "she turned to Mr. Little.

"I am not an expert in pearls, Miss Rosemary, I should not like to express an opinion. A very large sum, that is quite certain."

"What do you call a large sum? Fifty pounds?"

"My dear young lady! What are your notions of value. Multiply that by a hundred."

"Gawks!" said Rosemary, awestruck, hastily handing the necklace over to her mother lest harm should befall it.

CHAPTER XIII

AS any one who has been in an accident knows, shock is its own anaesthetic. Stella went about in a kind of daze, paying no attention to anything, and if she had been asked, would have said that she felt nothing. She was not nagged, as Mr. Hope had strictly forbidden any reference to the débâcle; it was just as if it had never happened; in fact, Stella almost began to think it had never happened but that she had just read of it somewhere.

As usual, references to Li cropped up in conversation, and for a moment the old wound woke up and ached, but it soon sank into numbness again. All the same, she knew it was a crippling wound, and that she would carry its scars to her grave.

She learnt, to her very great relief, that Li had not given way to another 'binge' or its equivalent. It was thought at first that he was, as euphemistically put by Mr. Mathers, 'off on the bust again,' for he was neither at Pei-Chi nor in his flat over the bank: then it was learnt that he was stopping with Mr. Mc-Culloch, who was also a bachelor with a flat over his business premises. Speculation was rife as to why he was doing this.

"Nervous breakdown," said Rosemary with a knowing grin, "McCulloch's holding his hand."

Her father silenced her with a glare that even she could not face.

"It's quite likely," said Mr. Mathers. "You know what these southern Chinese are like when they go in off the deep end."

So Stella found what comfort she could in knowing that Li had really cared, and that McCulloch was looking after him.

The lease of the Hope Navigation Co.'s wharf was still unsigned, and they were going on as annual tenants subject to a quarter's notice, an uneasy position for a big firm; but Li did not seem disposed to take advantage of it. Mrs. Hope was terrified that he was merely biding his time, but Mr. Mathers, who by virtue of his office as editor knew a great deal more than ever appeared in his paper, reassured her.

"As far as I can make out," he said, "Li has gone completely into abeyance. Cut his loss over Stella, don't you know, and decided to make the best of a bad job. I think it's hit him pretty hard, and now it's over, there's no fight left in him. That's how it looks to me. You know what these chaps are like—go absolutely on the rampage, and then are all in and dead to the wide. Li's dead to the wide now, believe me, if looks are anything to go by. I caught sight of him the other day, and he's put on ten years over-night. I feel quite sorry for the chap, though, of course, the situation was an impossible one, and he's just as well out of it as Miss Stella is. There's no kick coming from him, don't you worry about that, Robert."

"Well, there's a kick or two coming from me, if there's any trouble," said Mr. Hope grimly.

The tame cat rose to take his leave.

"Cheer up, Miss Stella," he said, shaking her warmly by the hand. "There are as good fish in the sea as ever came out of it."

She smiled drearily as she bid him good-bye, for she would be sailing before they saw him again; there might be good fish in the sea, as he said, but her tackle had carried away.

On his return to the office after lunch, Mr. Hope had a visitor that surprised him. It was none other than Mr. McCulloch.

"I have come on rather a delicate errand," he said.

Mr. Hope's ears went back metaphorically, and he braced himself for resistance.

"I feel some embarrassment in opening the subject with you," said his visitor, "but I think my intervention may save a very great deal of unpleasantness. I am perfectly satisfied that an explanation will be forthcoming, and I considered that the biggest service I could do you, as an old friend, was to come straight to you and ask you to entrust me with that explanation so that I may put things right for you."

"What is it?" said Mr. Hope, grimly and not very graciously.

"I may as well tell you that I have heard the story of this unhappy business between your niece and Li Wu Lu. I understand that he gave her a pearl necklace—please realise that there is no question of his wanting the return of that necklace, he is only too pleased for her to keep it—but it has come to his knowledge that the necklace is being broken up and sold piecemeal; moreover, it is not being sold by Miss Morris, but by some one else, and he regards the circumstances of the sale as peculiar. He wants to satisfy himself that Miss Morris is not being taken advantage of, that is all."

"Good Lord!" exclaimed Mr. Hope. "That necklace was supposed to have been returned to Li. My wife was seeing to it."

"How did she send it?"

"I've no idea. By one of the servants I expect. I'll have the matter looked into. Will you tell Li how extremely sorry we are."

"I had better tell you the full facts, Hope—it is your wife who is selling it."

"My God, McCulloch, what are you suggesting?"

"I am not suggesting anything. I am sure there is a perfectly satisfactory explanation, and have told Li so. He is not vindictive; all he says is: All right, let me have that explanation. As long as he is satisfied that Miss Morris is benefiting by the sale of the pearls, he will be perfectly happy; he has got it fixed in his head that she isn't, and nothing will budge that idea, and unless he is satisfied on that point, he will make trouble. What I want you to do is to meet him and explain the situation."

"I can't explain the situation, I know no more about it than you do, possibly less. Florence will have to explain it."

"Will you send for her?"

"What, now?

"Yes, now. Li's got the insurance assessor and a pearl expert over at my place waiting to see what answer I get from you. The thing will be in the hands of the police this evening if we can't

166

pacify him."

"My God, we've got to pacify him! I'll get Florence down at once."

He picked up the desk telephone and put through a call to his house. Knowing the ways of local exchanges, he would not be specific on the phone, and it took a lot of wrangling and some bullying to convince Mrs. Hope that she must cut an appointment with her dressmaker and come down town right away; to all of which Mr. McCulloch listened with an expression of profound distaste. Then they sat down to await her arrival.

She did not keep them waiting long, as she still hoped to be able to manage the visit to her dressmaker.

"Well, and what's it all about?" she exclaimed as she came sailing into the room. Her husband told her. It was impossible to see whether she changed colour under her make-up, but her voice sounded very queer when she replied. Nevertheless, her words were reassuring.

"Is Li suggesting that I have stolen the necklace from Stella?" she asked tartly.

"Apparently," said her husband. "But what I want to know is, why it hasn't gone back to Li?"

"The answer to that is very simple, Stella wouldn't part with it when it came to the point. She said, which is quite true, that you were proposing to pack her back to Europe without a penny, and she'd starve; whereas this necklace would save her bacon. Li hadn't asked for it back, so why send it back ? It seemed to me pretty reasonable, but I didn't like to tell you because I knew you would go in off the deep end; so I undertook to peddle the necklace for the child as I knew the ropes better than she did, and would get a better price than she would."

"It is a great pity that you are peddling it piecemeal, Mrs. Hope," said Mr. McCulloch. "It loses enormously in value when broken up."

"So I told Stella," replied Mrs. Hope, "but she wanted to keep as much of it as she could for sentimental reasons."

"Very well, then," said Mr. McCulloch, "we had better go

across and let you tell Li that; it ought to satisfy him."

Mrs. Hope suddenly clutched at the arm of her chair.

"You don't want me to see Li, do you?" she cried breathlessly. "Won't it be enough if you tell him?"

"I am afraid not. He insists on a personal interview. He wishes to ask certain questions himself."

"Sorry, Florence, but I'm afraid you'll have to go through with it. Li will make himself damned unpleasant if you don't. This is what comes of doing things behind my back."

"Oh dear. Must I? How can he make himself unpleasant?"

"He is threatening to put the matter in the hands of the police."

"But how can he do that? He gave the necklace to Stella; she can sell it if she wants to."

"I don't know how he can do it, not having had legal advice, but that's what he says he'll do. He may be bluffing—I don't know; but anyway, he means to make a damned stink if he isn't pacified, so you had better come along and pacify him. He's a very great friend of yours and you can do anything with him— or so you're always telling everybody."

"Oh dear, I suppose I'll have to; but I do hate seeing him again after all that's happened. You know he nearly murdered us, don't you, Mr. McCulloch?"

"Yes, I do. How you ever got alive out of that house is a miracle."

Mrs. Hope looked startled. She had not believed her own statement when she made it, but was merely being sensational. To find that it was true was no small shock to her.

She rose, and they went out through the main office to walk the few yards to McCulloch's bank. Outside the door of the Hope premises they saw Stella sitting in the Daimler, gazing out over the harbour with unseeing eyes. She did not notice them, and Mrs. Hope was about to pass quietly by without attracting her attention. But Mr. McCulloch stopped her.

"We shall want Miss Morris," he said.

"No, no, don't do that," said Mrs. Hope hastily in an undertone. "She has been terribly upset over this business. It would be disastrous for them to meet again."

"I am entirely of your opinion, Mrs. Hope, and have done my best to convince Li on that point, but he won't have it. He insists on hearing from Miss Morris's own lips that she is bene-fiting by the disposal of the necklace, and that no coercion has been brought to bear on her."

Mrs. Hope made no reply, but leant heavily on her sun shade, and Mr. McCulloch went up to the door of the Daim-ler, rested his hands on it, and bent down to speak to the girl within. She looked up, startled, seeing everything go round for a minute, for it was exactly the attitude assumed by another man who had wished to speak to her while she had sat in that car, and at that very moment she had been thinking of him.

McCulloch did not explain to her what she was really want-ed for at his bank, but contented himself with telling her that she was needed in connection with the pearl necklace that had been placed in her possession. She bowed her head and got out as bidden. He saw by her face that what he had said conveyed little or nothing to her.

She followed her aunt through the public part of the China Scottish Bank, and up the handsome stairs to the general man-ager's office. As she came through the doorway in the wake of her aunt, she caught her breath, for she saw Li across the room at the far side of a huge table. But with him were two other men, strangers to her, so she knew that nothing sentimental was afoot.

Li looked up for one brief second, met her eyes, then looked down again. They took their places round the table as if for a directors' meeting. McCulloch at the head with Li on his right; on his left the two strangers, both Jews: then there was a gap, and Mr. Hope sat facing him at the foot of the table, with his wife on his right and his niece on his left. Consequently Stella could only see Li side-face, but that brief glance told her that Mr. Mathers had been right when he had said that Li looked ten years older and all the fight had gone out of him.

Mr. McCulloch took charge of the interview. Li never raised his eyes, but steadily stabbed at a blotter with a pen till it looked as if mice had been at it. The two Jews were evidently not expected to speak till they were spoken to.

"As Miss Morris has not heard the story, I will recapitulate it briefly for her benefit," said Mr. McCulloch. "We understand that she had in her possession a pearl necklace of no inconsiderable value. A certain pearl from that necklace has been sold by a person other than herself. The insurance company responsible for that necklace wish to know whether she authorised the sale. Mr. Hyams here represents the insurance company."

Stella raised her eyes to meet the keen dark ones of the Jewish assessor that were fixed steadily on her.

"I know nothing about it," she said. "I never authorised any sale. I gave the necklace to my aunt to send back to—the person who gave it to me."

"That is a lie," said Mrs. Hope. " It is true that Stella gave it me once, but she took it back again and asked me to sell one of the pearls for her so that she might have some ready money."

"Oh, Aunt Florence, I didn't. How can you say such a thing!" cried Stella indignantly.

"I certainly do," said Mrs. Hope calmly. "And they can please themselves whom they believe. It is your word against mine, and with your somewhat unsavoury record, I fancy it is mine that will be accepted by my friends."

"Vell, not qvite, madam," said the Jewish assessor. "Dere's a lot more dan folks' vords to it. Can you tell us how it is dat der bank-notes, vot you vood have instead of a cheque, are comin' into der banks from vine-merchants, dressmakers, bookies, and such-like, and dey say dey got dem in settlement of your accounts vith dem?"

"My God, Li, you didn't tell me that!" exclaimed McCulloch.

"No," said Li without looking up. "You whites all hang together."

"Hope, I can't tell you how sorry I am that this has been sprung on you. I would never have been a party to leading you into a trap if I had known," exclaimed McCulloch, very agitated.

"No fault of yours, McCulloch, I'm sure," replied Mr. Hope. "It's got to be faced. Where is the rest of the necklace, Florence?"

"I'm sure I don't know. You'd better ask Stella."

"It's not I who will ask Stella, it's the police will ask Stella if you play the fool any more. Come clean, the game's up. Can't you see that McCulloch and I will help you out if we can? For God's sake, come clean for all our sakes."

Sulkily Mrs. Hope put her hand inside her dress and drew out the mangled necklace, the severed ends of the silk thread tied in a clumsy knot where the great centre pearl had been. She laid it on the table. The pearl-dealer took a small package out of his pocket, where he appeared to be carrying it loose, unfolded it with a skilful twist of finger and thumb, and laid the great pearl in her place beside her sisters.

"Thank God for that," said Mr. Hope with a sigh of relief. "What do I owe you, Li? I'll pay you back what Florence got for it."

"No, you won't," said Li, his mouth working nervously.

"You'll pay Stella back. It's her necklace."

"Na, na, chentlemans," intervened the pearl-dealer, "you can't settle it dot vay. Der chentleman vot bought der pearl from Mrs. Hope vill vant his little bit. He von't be content to take vhat he give. Now if Mrs. Hope had come to me——"

"What did he give?" Mr. Hope cut him short bluntly.

"Five 'undred."

"Dollars?"

"Na-a-h, sterling!" the Jew's snarl expressed unutterable contempt.

"Five hundred pounds for the one pearl? Well, what does he want to buy it back again?"

"Two thousand—sterling."

"Good God, is it worth that?

"Ya. Dat vas vot ye should have insured her for if ve had gone on vith the deal."

"My Lord! Then what's the necklace worth complete?"

"Twenty thousand—sterling. There ain't never been no

necklace like her. Dot pearl, she vas der qveen, I spent all my life matchin' her. Den, yen she vas matched, dere vas only von man east of Suez to buy 'er—'im." He jerked his thumb at the silent and abstracted Li, who paid no manner of attention to him.

Suddenly Mrs. Hope began to giggle hysterically.

"You cannot do anything!" she cried excitedly. "That necklace is Stella's. The only person who can do anything is Stella, and she daren't, because if it becomes known that she took a twenty thousand pound present from Li—well—she's finished, isn't she?"

"I'll do whatever Mr. Li says," said Stella, in a low voice, "it's his necklace."

"What's the good of his saying anything? He can't do anything. He can't claim that necklace back again after giving it to you."

"As a matter of fact, I can," said Li without looking up, "but I don't wish to as long as it is applied for Miss Morris's benefit. It was given her in anticipation of marriage, the marriage is not coming off, therefore I could claim its return if I wanted to; and I will, too, if it is necessary in her interest."

"But it was you who broke off the engagement, not her."

"No, it wasn't."

"It was. I saw the letter."

Li looked up. "What letter?"

"Yours to her—"

"You can't read Chinese, you don't know what that letter contained."

"I read the translation of it Robert had made at the office."

Li rose slowly to his feet. " Is that right, Stella ? Did you get a letter from me breaking off the engagement?"

"Yes," said Stella miserably.

"Do you happen to have it on you?"

She thrust her hand into the front of her dress and drew out two crumpled sheets of paper—the Chinese letter on the headed paper of the Inland and Overseas Bank, and its

English translation on the paper of the Hope Navigation Company. Li leant over and took them from her, unfolded them, and laid them flat on the table in their midst. Stella saw that his hands were shaking so that he could hardly handle them. Then he drew out his own pocket-book, opened it, and took out a letter in Chinese script, but on the headed paper of Esperanza House. He laid it beside the others.

"Any of you gentlemen read Chinese?" " he asked.

The two Jews and McCulloch nodded. Li passed the letters to them. They read them one by one and passed them on.

"Well, what do you say?"

"Vell, dey's der same letter," said the pearl dealer. "Just der names is different, dat's all. She breaks off her engagement vith you, and you does it vith her, in the same vords—or some vun does it for you."

Li drew out a revolver.

"Everybody keep still," he said, "there is no danger, I shall not use it unless I am forced to."

He walked round the table till he came to the back of Mr. Hope's chair. Nobody stirred, nor was there any sound save a little hysterical gulping from Mrs. Hope. Then he bent over and cuffed Mr. Hope good and hard.

"There, take that! " he said. "Tell your friends you have had your face smacked by a Chink—and remember it yourself."

Then he walked back to his chair as quietly as he had come, sat down, and laid his revolver on the table before him. Still nobody moved, for the revolver had the safety catch raised.

"Now I will tell you my terms," he said. "Firstly, you will give your consent to my marriage with your niece."

"I shall do nothing of the sort," said Mr. Hope.

"I am not speaking to you. She is not your niece, she is your wife's niece. I want your consent, Mrs. Hope."

"And supposing I won't give it, what then?"

"Then I shall claim against the insurance company for the loss of the pearl necklace."

"Well, and what will happen if you do? There is the necklace, in front of you. It isn't lost."

"But the centre pearl is not in the necklace any longer."

"Well, put it back. If you can tie a knot in a piece of string, you can put it back. There it is."

"May I do that, Mr. Berg?"

"Nab, you may not. Dot pearl, she is entrusted to me as broker by der man vot bought her."

"He bought stolen goods."

"You got to prove dat."

"How am I to prove it?"

"Prove der identity of der pearl."

"Yes, there you are," chimed in Mrs. Hope, "how are you going to prove that? How do you know it isn't my pearl, that I had a perfect right to sell?"

"You claim dot?" " Mr. Hyams chipped in.

"Er, yes," said Mrs. Hope a little uncertainly. "I—er—I claim that—yes."

"You qvite sure?"

"Er, yes, I'm quite sure."

"Very veil. Now den, Mr. Berg." He opened a despatch case and took out a bulky document. Mr. Berg dived into one of his innumerable pockets and produced a shabby old notebook. Mr. Hyams unfurled his document and ran his finger down column after column of fine writing.

"Dis is her, der big von in der middle. Now den, Mr. Berg, you got her?"

"Ya, I got her. Now den, Mr. Hyams."

They began to check, point by point, item by item, the features of the great pearl. Every pimple, dimple, pin-spot or shadow on any big pearl are listed by every man through whose hands she has passed since the diver brought her up from the bed of the sea. Mrs. Hope grew limper and limper as she heard that catalogue. It was short, for the great pearl was as nearly perfect as anything in Nature ever is.

"Ve are agreed?" said Mr. Hyams, at the end of the brief recital.

"Ve are agreed," said Mr. Berg.

"Dot pearl vot Mr. Li insured with us, she vos sold by you to

Mr. Li?"

"Und vere did you get her?"

"I vos on der lugger ven she come up. I remember it like a man remember his first love, She vos der first big pearl I ever bought on my own. I vos tventy-three. I am fifty-three now. Thirty year I bin makin' dot string."

"Now den, vot about dis here pearl, vot ye got here?"

Point by point the two men checked the great pearl against their respective lists. Then out came a little pair of fine balances from Mr. Berg's ubiquitous pockets, and the pearl was weighed against the infinitesimal weights.

"Ya, dot's her," said Mr. Berg.

The assessor turned to Mrs. Hope.

"Now den, Mrs. Hope, you say dot pearl is your pearl. Vell, vere did you get her?"

Mrs. Hope sat speechless, slowly tearing her handkerchief to pieces.

"Now den, Mrs. Hope, you goin' to answer my question?"

"I won't have my wife spoken to like that," Mr. Hope intervened sharply.

"Very good," said Mr. Hyams, beginning to put away his papers.

"She had better answer, Hope," said Mr. McCuiloch quietly.

"She needn't," came the voice of Li Wu Lu even more quietly.

Mrs. Hope turned to him like a hunted animal seeing a chance of escape.

"No, you needn't answer that question unless you want to, Mrs. Hope. I do not wish to press it."

"Oh, that is nice of you, Mr. Li. Of course we will make everything all right about the pearl."

"Yes, I am sure you will and now, about my marriage to your niece? You consent?"

"Er, no, I am very sorry, Mr. Li, but I am really afraid I can't."

"Then—" said Li, his face suddenly changing into the devil-

175

mask Stella was beginning to know so well, "answer Mr. Hyams' question!"

Mrs. Hope sat biting what was left of her handkerchief between her teeth.

"You have no option, Mrs. Hope," said Mr. McCulloch in a low voice.

She turned to her husband. "What shall I do, Robert?"

"Do what you damn well please. It is your folly that has let us all in for this."

"Oh, very well, then, I'll consent, but it is rotten for Rosemary. You can marry Stella, Mr. Li. I'll expect you'll treat her as she deserves, and it serves her right."

"Dere now, dot's all happily settled," said Mr. Berg, beaming at every one. "Now den, Mr. Hope, dere's only der leedle cheque for my friend, and ve're through."

"The little cheque?"

"Ya, for two thousand."

"But this is blackmail."

"No, it ain't. Dot's der proper price for dot pearl. Me, I fixed it. I'm der honest broker. I don't let 'im black mail you. Not yet, anyvay; 'e may presently ven I'm gone; 'e's dot sort. Mrs. Hope, she don't choose a 'igh class man for 'er business—and perhaps she's right."

Mr. Hope drew out his cheque-book and wrote out the cheque without a word.

"Make it open," said Mr. Berg. He picked up the cheque that was handed to him, endorsed it, and passed it across to Mr. McCulloch. McCulloch held it in his hand for a long minute, looking at Mr. Hope, then, without a word, he passed it back to him. There was dead silence round the table.

Mr. Hope hesitated, then drew another cheque-book out of his pocket, wrote another cheque, and flung it across to McCulloch. The banker examined it.

"You realise what you are doing, Hope?" he asked.

"Yes, I'll make it all right to-morrow."

"Well, of course I have nothing to say, whatever I may think. The funds are there to meet it, you are authorised to sign, and it must be met."

He pressed a bell, a clerk entered, and he sent him down to cash the cheque.

"That lets Mrs. Hope out," said Li, pocketing his revolver.

"Now I will deal with you, Hope."

"Mr. Hope to you, please."

"Hein, a rose by any name smells just as sweet, and manure smells just as nasty. Why worry? You are going to sell me your business, Mr. Hope, at my price, without haggling. Yes or no, take it or leave it. My price is a hundred and seventy-two thousand. Do you call that fair, Mr. Hyams? You are well up in these things."

"No, 'tain't fair, not by a long chalk. 'Tain't fair to you. He ain't got no lease. His show is only vorth vhat his boats 'll fetch at auction, and they're bum boats, ye all know dot."

"I do not wish to see a family I am related to in the gutter. I will pay him a fair price. That is my offer, Mr. Hope. Will you take it and go, or will you stop on and fight to a finish?"

"For God's sake take it, Hope," muttered Mr. McCulloch.

"No one else will give you that price without a lease."

"Damned if I will !" shouted the ship-owner. "I've got a shot or two in my locker yet. I'm not so stuck for a lease as you think."

"Well, you know your own business best. I shall be asking you to reduce your overdraft, though. I'm not carrying you if you are going to play the skin game with Li."

"Very well, then," said Li, rising. "I think we have settled all outstanding points. You will not sell, and I, who have a mind to go into the shipping business, must make other arrangements."

Mr. Hope rose, and without a word of farewell to any one, stalked towards the door, followed by his wife. Stella rose too, and stood hesitating whether to follow them or not. Her uncle turned at the sound and looked at her, said one filthy word, and walked out of the door.

"I will bankrupt you for that, Hope," Li called after him.

Stella stood looking helplessly from one to the other of the men who remained. The name she had been called had struck her like a blow in the face, and she felt unspeakably soiled and shamed—as if she would never be able to hold up her head again.

It was the little Jew pearl dealer who saved the situation. He came round the table and took her hand and shook it warmly.

"Now den, Mees Morris, you vill let me be der first to congratulate you? I tink you are a very lucky girl. You have got a real good man. You make him a good vife, and you viii have nothing to grumble at. And venever I get anything ver' goot, I vill bring it round, and he vill give it you. Now I haf got dis at der moment—" He dived into his pockets again, and produced another twist of paper, flicked it open skilfully, and revealed two perfectly matched pink pear-shaped pearls.

"Rosée-rosée, same as der necklace. Vot you say to dem for ear-rings? " He held one up against Stella's creamy cheek. "Dey look fine, don't dey? Yes? No? Vot you say, Mr. Li? Ain't dot a grand skin to put pearls on? Der diamonds—no, dey ain't for her. But der pearls now, der rosée pearls. She should collect dem. She should have a parure for der hair. Und anoder string of pearls, short, close up to der neck, und den a long von, right down to her middle. Und I haf at home a button pearl, also rosée-rosée, for der ring. Ya, she is made for der pink pearls, und der pink pearls is made for her."

Li shook his head. "I can't cope with pearls at the moment," he said.

The dealer turned to Stella. "You like dem, eh, Miss Morris?"

"I think they are very lovely," said Stella, "but I cannot cope with pearls either at the moment."

The little Jew sighed, and sadly folded up his treasures in their bit of paper.

"I never seed a skin more vorthy of pearls," he said, "and I do not say dat just because I am a dealer. No von vill see dese pearls till you haf had der chance to make up your mind."

The two Jews took their leave. As soon as they were gone, McCulloch turned to Li.

"You ought to have been frank with me," he said.

"If I had been frank with you, you wouldn't have done what I wanted."

"All the more reason for being frank with me."

"I fail to see it. I didn't mislead you. It was you who insisted that the yellow man's suspicions of the white woman were groundless. You never asked what grounds I had for my suspicions. It was enough for you that she was white and I was coloured."

"Oh, don't start off on that tack again."

"Is that also groundless? Let us test it. Knowing what you know, will you help me checkmate Hope's spite so that my marriage with Stella has a chance of success?"

McCulloch was silent.

"No, you won't," said Li. "All the same, I don't think you'll let him increase his overdraft. A Scotchman's friendship, even for another white man, won't stretch to that. But if the positions were reversed, and you were in his shoes, and banking at my bank, I would let you overdraw for everything I was good for, and go smash with you, if necessary."

"You have put me in an extremely awkward position."

"In what way?"

"It must look to Hope as if I had ratted on him."

"Well, won't you, now that you know the facts?"

"What facts?"

"The stealing of the necklace from Stella, and the forging of those letters."

"The—er—matter of the necklace was, of course, unpardonable, I have not a word to say in defence of Mrs. Hope's conduct, either at the time or when things began to come out. But in the matter of the letters—I expect Hope thought he was acting for the best."

"If you had known about those letters, McCulloch, would you have come to me in the same way that you went to Hope when you knew about the sale of the pearl?"

"I don't know what I should have done, Li. I don't like forgery any better than you do, but I don't like a mixed marriage either, and I certainly wouldn't have helped you to it."

179

"When I went to pieces, did you take me to your flat because you were sorry for me in my trouble, or because you wanted to prevent me from letting hell loose on the Concession?"

McCulloch did not answer.

"Yes," said Li, "I was right when I took that oath never to make a friend of a white man. Come, Stella," and he turned towards the door.

McCulloch walked across and barred the way. He put his hand on Stella's shoulder.

"My dear," he said, "are you going into this marriage of your own free will, or have you been coerced in any way?"

"I'll kill you if you come between us," said Li through his teeth, his hand going to his hip.

"No," said Stella, "I have not been coerced in any way."

"Not that night at Pei-Chi?"

"No, not even then." A little smile curled the corners of Stella's mouth. "If you want to know the truth, it was I who coerced Li Wu Lu. You see, I thought he needed looking after."

"And you thought you were the person to undertake that?"

"I seem to be the only person who can manage him. He seems to want to murder everybody else."

"You realise what you are doing?"

"No, I'm afraid I don't. I've never been married before."

She caught Li's eye over his shoulder; he began to laugh and took his hand away from his revolver.

McCulloch turned round at the sound. He looked from one of them to the other.

"Yes," he said, "I see you can manage him."

"Hein, Mac," said Li, "will you be Stella's trustee for the settlement I want to make on her?"

McCulloch looked at him over his spectacles.

"I see your game perfectly clearly," he said. "Don't think you can throw dust in my eyes. You want to make me appear to approve of your marriage to Miss Morris. Well, I don't approve of your marriage to Miss Morris, and I've told you so; but if there is anything I can do to mitigate the consequences of it, I will. Yes, I will be Miss Morris's trustee, and if you play any hanky-panky, God help you, young fellow, and that is all I have to say."

He turned to Stella. "I want to talk to Li Wu Lu," he said. "He needs a talking-to, and now's the time to do it. Will you wait downstairs in the banking hall, my dear?"

CHAPTER XIV

STELLA came down the broad stairs into the public part of the bank and looked round for something to sit on while she was waiting. Banks are not lavish with their seating accommodation, money not being a thing in which there is much chance to exercise taste. She saw near the door a single bench of the variety that is used at school treats, handsomely carried out in mahogany. This seat of little ease was already occupied by a woman, but there was plenty of room for two if the one moved up, and Stella went towards it.

The woman, her eyes anxiously fixed on the door of the manager's office, did not notice her approach, and made no move to make room for her.

"Do you mind if I share your seat while I wait?" said Stella to her.

She looked up, startled.

"Oh, it's Miss Morris," she said. "I'm so sorry, I didn't see you. Yes, do sit down," and she moved to make room.

"I know you quite well by sight," she went on as Stella sat down. "You're Mrs. Hope's niece, aren't you. I have wanted to meet you, but somehow it never came about; we are not in the Hopes' set. We are never even asked to the omnium gatherings."

"I am very pleased indeed to meet you," said Stella. "But I am afraid I don't even know you by sight."

"I am Mrs. Conyers, Mrs. Gerald Conyers, to be precise my husband is the 'and Son' of John Conyers and Son.

"We are Mr. Hope's least formidable rivals."

Then Stella knew who she was. She knew, too, why she had been gazing at the door of the manager's office with such anxious eyes—her husband, the young, inexperienced and Son,' was in there, trying to get an overdraft. Mr. Hope had been certain he would try for it, and had been equally certain that he wouldn't get it. Old John Conyers, smitten with a stroke, lay speechless and helpless, and the boy was trying to carry on as best he might, and Mr. Hope and his friends, believing in the good old maxim 'dog eat dog,' were not being helpful. She had heard Mr. Mathers, who was very friendly with the Conyers, try to put in a plea for mercy, only to be snorted to scorn. Pretty, witty, young Mrs. Conyers was the leading light of the younger intellectuals, mockingly called 'the Souls,' just as Mrs. Hope was the leading light of the sporting, moneyed set. The Souls were unpopular with Mrs. Hope because one of them had snaffled a diplomat on whom she had had her eye for Rosemary.

At one time there was nothing that Stella would have liked better than to get in with the Souls, among whom she was sure that she would have been able to make friends, but what would they have to say to her as the wife of a Chinaman?

She returned Mrs. Conyers' lead politely but without enthusiasm lest she should lay herself open to the painful experience of being taken up and dropped.

Mrs. Conyers, quick in the uptake, sensed that the lack of warmth in the girl's response did not come from any lack of cordiality, but that for some reason she hesitated to accept the proffered friendship.

"Never mind the family feud. Need we take sides in that? I am sure I should like you if I knew you," she said.

"I didn't know there was a family feud," said Stella.

"Didn't you? Well, there's no secret about it on our side. Your uncle is trying to squeeze my husband out. He wants our wharf. It's like King David and Bathsheba, if that's the lady's name, He's got that great big wharf of his, and yet he wants our little one."

"Oh, does he?" said Stella, thinking hard.

At that moment the door of the manager's office opened, and Gerald Conyers came out. He did not need to speak to announce his news. The way he crossed the floor was enough.

"Nothing doing?" said his wife, looking up at him.

He shook his head without speaking.

They looked at each other for a moment.

"If there is any justice under heaven, Hope ought to get it in the neck for this," said Gerald Conyers bitterly.

"He will," said Stella. "Don't you worry."

They turned and looked at her in surprise.

"I thought you said you didn't know anything about the family feud?" said Mrs. Conyers.

"I don't—not about your feud, but I know about another my uncle has got on his hands."

"Are you Miss Morris?" said Gerald Conyers. "I thought I knew your face. You live with the Hopes, don't you?"

"I did."

"Oh, aren't you there any longer?" asked Mrs. Conyers.

"No."

"Where are you now?"

"Sitting on this seat."

"Yes, but where are you living?"

"I don't know,"

"But you must be living somewhere."

"I'm not. I'm just sitting on this seat."

"Good Lord, have the Hopes chucked you out?" exclaimed Gerald Conyers.

"No, they haven't chucked me out, but I know better than to go back after something that has just happened."

"Do you care to tell us what it is? Perhaps we can help you," said Mrs. Conyers.

Stella hesitated. She was not sure whether Li was ready for publicity just yet.

"I am awfully sorry, but I'm afraid I can't. You see, it doesn't concern me only."

"Right, we won't press you," said Mrs. Conyers, "but would you care to come back with us until you have a chance to look round?"

Stella hesitated again. "I'd like to awfully, but I don't think I ought to involve you in my problems. You mightn't like them if you knew what they were."

"Are they so very terrible?"

"I don't think so. I think I am doing the right thing, but you mightn't."

At that moment a door opened and the two Jews appeared, returning from the vaults where they had been depositing the pearls. The assessor, with a bow to Stella, hurried out, but the pearl dealer came towards her.

"Dere now, Miss Morris, your two pearls is in der vaults, and dey vill stop dere till you are ready to look at dem. You ought to ask for dose pearls for a vedding present. You get dem all right. You'd get anyting YOU liked to ask for out of dat man. I never seed anyvon got it so badly."

"Your pearls are perfectly lovely, Mr. Berg, but I don't want to cadge."

"No, I know you don't. You ain't after him for vot you can get out of him. You're real fond of him, ain't you? I seed dat. Mr. Hyams, he tink you been druv to it, but I don't. Vel, I vish you luck. You'll need it. I know someting about dese 'ere race feelin's. I used to be a Cherman, I vos. An' before dat, my folk, dey come from der Ukraine. I vos born in a pogrom, I vos. I vish yer luck. You got a friend in me. No, an' I don't say dat to sell no pearls, neider."

Mrs. Conyers looked at the girl beside her as the little Jew hurried after his friend.

"Is your problem a mixed marriage?" she asked.

"Yes," said Stella.

"A Chinese?"

"Yes."

"Well, our invitation still holds good, doesn't it, Gerald? We don't go in for race prejudices. Some of our best friends are Chinese. A good Chinese is the salt of the earth. A man like Li Wu Lu, for instance, the man who owns the other big bank—" and then, suddenly remembering her own troubles, which had been put aside for the moment in her interest in Stella, she turned to her husband.

"Gerald, why don't you try Li's bank?"

"No, Monica, it's not the slightest use. If our own bank won't do it, it can't be done."

They looked to each other silently, Stella's presence forgotten.

"Won't Hope take you over with the company?" said Monica Conyers.

"Don't think so. He won't say, anyway. I tried to bargain for that, but he won't bargain. He just says those are his terms; take them or leave them."

Stella spoke, and at the sound of her voice, they turned with a start, having almost forgotten she was there.

"Do you know that I have just heard those very words used to my uncle? I don't believe he will be in a position to twist your tail for very long, Mr. Conyers. He's going to have a taste of tail-twisting himself."

"That won't help me very much, Miss Morris, I'm afraid. I've got to find the debenture interest by tomorrow morning or he puts the receiver in. First he puts on folk to take up our debenture issue for him in small parcels, here and there, so that we don't suspect; then he cuts the freight rates below cost; and then he won't give an hour's grace on the debenture interest. It's not a pretty game, but it's perfectly legal. Well, there's no point in stopping here any longer, we may as well go home—while we've got a home. Care to come along, Miss Morris? You're very welcome if you do, and your fiancé too."

At that moment Li appeared on the stairs leading from McCulloch's office.

"Is that your fiancé?" said Mrs. Conyers.

"Don't you know the famous Li Wu Lu when you see him?" said her husband, before Stella could reply.

"No, I'm afraid I don't; I can't tell one Chinaman from another," said Mrs. Conyers.

Li came down the wide shallow stairs with that supple, cat-like movement that Stella had come to know so well, and with the immense dignity of imperturbable self-possession that he shared with the cat tribe, The only person who had ever been able to shake him out of that self-possession was Stella.

He crossed the wide tessellated floor and approached the little group gathered about the hard bench and bowed to them, greeting Gerald Conyers by name. Gerald, immensely flattered at being greeted thus, for he occupied a very different position in life to the Chinese millionaire, introduced him to his wife and Stella. He bowed to both impartially. Stella wondered what in the world he was up to now, for it was hopeless to try to keep their prospective marriage secret any longer. However, she judged it best to follow his lead, and returned his bow as formally as it had been given.

A clock overhead boomed four, and before they could do more than exchange the merest formalities, a commissionaire came and shepherded them out of the bank and shut the door behind them.

Drawn up outside was a shabby little baby car. Mrs. Conyers turned to Stella.

"Well, Miss Morris, what do you want to do? Will you come home with us? You are very welcome."

Stella hesitated, and her eyes sought Li's for a second.

He picked up his cue.

"I suppose you know the dreadful faux pas Miss Morris is committing?" he said.

Mrs. Conyers bristled. "I beg your pardon?"

"You know Miss Morris is making a mixed marriage with a Chinaman?"

"Is it your business, Mr. Li, who Miss Morris marries? Or whom I ask to my house?"

"It is not my business who you ask to your house, but it is my business who Miss Morris marries."

"Why?"

"Because I happen to be the Chinaman she is marrying."

"Is that so? Is that really so?" exclaimed Mrs. Conyers delightedly, turning to Stella. "Why ever didn't you tell us?"

"Because I wasn't sure whether Li Wu Lu wanted it announced just yet, so I thought it was better to let him tell you."

"And are we the first to know? How exciting. Is it a secret or may we talk? I do congratulate you most heartily, Mr. Li," and she held out her hand to him. He hesitated a moment, and then took it.

"That is very nice of you," he said. "Congratulations were not what I was expecting."

Gerald joined in the felicitations. Stella noticed that a man of the clerk type who was passing stared hard at all this hand-shaking. His face was vaguely familiar. She fancied he had once come to Esperanza House with papers from the office.

Li turned to Mrs. Conyers. "I did not know that you were friends of Stella's," he said.

"Neither did we, till this afternoon; but you can't share a seat like that one at the bank and not develop fellow-feeling," said Mrs. Conyers.

"And on the strength of sharing a seat, you ask Miss Morris to your home? That is no small thing to do, in the circumstances."

"Well, you see, I knew the Hopes, even if I didn't know her; and I knew how they would treat the child in the circumstances. I didn't know she was engaged to you, who would be in a position to look after her."

"Hein," said Li," I am grateful."

Silence fell between them for a moment. Then he turned to Stella.

"Well, my star, would you like to accept Mrs. Conyers' invitation? It will get us out of no small difficulty; I have been at my wits' end to know what to do with you, and could think of nothing save the Palace Hotel or the Y.W.C.A., neither of which I think you would have been very happy at under the circumstances."

Stella accepted gratefully, and Mrs. Conyers added an invitation to Li to come back to tea, which was also accepted.

They turned towards the shabby little car.

"I am afraid I can't take everybody," said Gerald Conyers. "She won't take the hill with more than two up."

"Shall I get my car? "said Li, "it is quite handy."

Gerald agreed with relief. "In that case," he said, "I will pop down to the wharf on my way back. They are a tally-clerk short down there."

So they separated. Stella, who badly wanted a word with Li, wondered how it was to be obtained, for the two women got into the wide back seat of the dust-grey limousine, and Li, who was driving himself, presented to them the back of a lacquer-black head.

Mrs. Conyers gave Stella's arm a squeeze.

"My dear, I am most awfully glad," she said.

"Are you really?" said Stella. "I thought there would be no end of a hue and cry after us."

"Not from my set. The Hopes' lot, yes, they'll shriek the place down; but ever since I've been out here I've worked at breaking down the barriers between East and West, and Gerald's people have done the same, too, all their lives. The folk you meet at our house won't hoot at you, Stella, or if they do, they won't be asked there again."

Then the swift, silent car turned into a pot-holed drive amid overgrown flowering shrubs, and they drew up at the shabby entrance to the Conyers' home, where, since the death of John Conyers' wife, young Mrs. Conyers had carried on the hospitable tradition of a welcome to any one who was worth knowing, without distinction of creed, caste or colour.

The hour for visits in that part of the world was the cocktail hour, between tea and dinner, after the day's work was over, on the way home from office or shopping as the case might be. That hour had not yet arrived, so there was no one save themselves in the big, homely, shabby drawing-room, the owner of the house lying log-like upstairs in the stupor of a stroke.

Li was as impassive and suavely impersonal as if he were paying an afternoon call and had found a fellow visitor in Stella. His impassiveness always chilled Stella, even though she knew what it was used to mask. Somehow she could never get it out of her head that when he was impassive he was estranged from her. The man himself seemed to recede and go a long way off, for the impassivity went deeper than the features, and he seemed to withdraw his whole personality.

Tea arrived, and Li, with perfect drawing-room manners,

did his part in passing cups and cakes. Stella, as usual when agitated, could not eat but was very thirsty, and drank her hot tea almost at a draught; but as the hot liquid passed down her throat, the over-taxed heart gave out, and she fell back among the cushions in a dead faint, the cup falling with a crash from her hand and shattering itself on the carpet.

There was one second's startled immobility on the part of the other two, and then Li sprang to his feet, crying some word aloud in Chinese that Mrs. Conyers could not understand, and caught Stella up bodily out of the chair as if she had been a baby. There he stood, his eyes blazing like a madman's, Stella's head with the long black hair fallen down, hanging limply over one arm and her knees hanging limply over the other.

"She has only fainted," cried Mrs. Conyers, "put her down and let us bring her round."

But there was nothing to be done with Li. He could only repeat the word he had already cried aloud, looking accusingly at the startled woman in front of him. All his English had gone from him, and he could neither speak nor understand any tongue save his own.

Mrs. Conyers hastily called the amah. At least she would be able to speak to Li in Chinese.

"He say she poisoned," said the amah.

"Oh no, nonsense, she's only fainted. Get him to put her down and we'll soon bring her round. We can't do anything while he clutches her like that."

After some persuasion, Li laid Stella down on the sofa, and then promptly flung himself on top of her. It was impossible to do anything with the fainting girl while the dead weight of a heavy man was on her chest, and Mrs. Conyers and the amah between them hauled him off. He sat up, his eyes blank and staring. Mrs. Conyers took him by the shoulders and shook him soundly.

That seemed to restore his wits.

"Is she dead?" he said.

"No, she's nothing of the sort. She's only fainted. You get out of the way and let us look after her," and she pushed Li forcibly off the sofa and got Stella straightened out. Once Li was off her chest, it was not the work of many minutes to bring her round, and she opened her eyes and looked up dazedly at them.

Then, seeing that her first patient was out of the wood, Mrs. Conyers turned her attention to her second one, to find that he was once more the suave, impassive Chinese business man, without a hair out of place. She gasped. She thought she knew the Chinese well, but she had not realised they were capable of this.

They heard the ringing of the front door bell, and knew that the first of the cocktailers was arriving.

She turned to Li. "Can YOU carry Stella upstairs for me?" she said, "we don't want folk to see all this, do we?"

He nodded, bent down, slipped his arms under Stella as she lay full length on the sofa, and picked her up as effortlessly as if she were a small child. Mrs. Conyers marvelled at the sinewy strength that lay hidden under the correctly cut office suit, for Li had none of the appearance of a strong man. She led the way, and he followed her up the wide shallow stairs, the amah pattering behind with Stella's oddments and his hat, so that no trace was left of the scene that had just taken place.

They arrived at the door of a little guest-room, and Mrs. Conyers threw back the coverlet from a low blue and white bed and bid Li lay Stella on it. But instead he stood motionless, gazing down into the face of the girl in his arms. Mrs. Conyers wondered how much longer he would go on holding Stella, for though she was petite, her weight was by no means negligible. It seemed as if he would stand there motionless indefinitely, and finally she touched his arm and again bade him lay the girl down.

"Hein, I beg your pardon," he said, coming to himself, and laid Stella on the bed as bid.

"That is the first time I have ever had Stella in my arms," he added.

Mrs. Conyers bid the amah fetch what was needed, and proceeded to shepherd Li out of the room. But Stella caught hold of his hand and would not let him go.

"I want to speak to him," she said. "I have not had a chance, I must speak to him."

"Won't it do in the morning?" said Mrs. Conyers.

"No, it won't," said Stella.

"Very good, only I shan't let you speak to him for long."

She withdrew, shutting the door behind her.

Li seated himself on the edge of the bed.

"Hein, Stella? What is it you want to speak to me about?"

His voice was very matter of fact, and as always, when he wore his mask of Chinese impassiveness, Stella felt chilled.

"Listen, Wu Lu," she said, her voice husky, for she was still feeling rather breathless, in spite of the brandy. " I have found out something important."

"What have you found out, my star?"

"I have found out the shot my uncle has in his locker, that he's always talking about—why he can afford to stand out against you—it's the Conyers' wharf."

She stopped, breathless, the room beginning to go round again.

"Is he in with the Conyers? "Li asked, sharply suspicious.

Stella shook her head, her voice not under control.

"Then—what is the game? How do the Conyers come into it?"

"He's—smashing them up," whispered Stella.

"Hein, my star, let me give you some more brandy. This is worrying you."

He poured her out a stiff peg.

Stella took firm hold on herself.

"They can't find the debenture interest, whatever that is."

"But Hope didn't take up their debentures."

"Yes, he did—through all sorts of folk."

"Hein," said Li thoughtfully, sitting on the edge of the bed with the bottle clasped in his hand. "That explains a lot."

The door opened, and Mrs. Conyers re-entered.

"If you two have done carousing—?" she said, seeing the brandy bottle in Li's hand.

"Hein, yes, I must go. I am doing her no good. But—that—was necessary, very necessary."

The delicate yellow fingers of his artist's hand touched Stella's cheek for a second.

"Come to me soon, my star," he said in a low voice.

Then he followed Mrs. Conyers out of the room without a glance behind him.

Mrs. Conyers handed him over to Gerald, who was dispensing cocktails to the assembled company. It was the day on which the Conyers held their gatherings, and the drinking of cocktails, coffee and beer, and the eating of all sorts of odd edibles with the fingers, or at most a fork, would go on till Gerald turned the lights down at midnight as a hint.

Li looked round him, considering the assembled company. There was a good sprinkling of Chinese, both men and women; there were some Jews, among whom was Mr. Berg. There was an old sea-captain, with a Chinese girl on one side of him and an English girl on the other, having a rollicking time with both impartially. There were a number of English and Americans from the colleges; some French and Russians from the legations, no Germans, and no commercial English.

The only person he knew in the room was Berg, until he saw Mathers coming through the door.

He smiled to himself at the sight, for he knew that the journalist had already been to the Hopes for some cocktails that really were cocktails before coming on to the Conyers' for the feast of reason and the flow of soul. Mr. Mathers might have a soul, but he also had a palate, and the fleshpots were dear to him; no one who kept a good table and asked him to it was ever pained by the columns of his paper. Gerald brought up an elderly Chinese doctor, whom Li knew by reputation, and introduced him. Li treated him with the elaborate deference that the Chinese always accord to age. The old man beamed. He was poor and shabby, but the great Li Wu Lu had not failed to give him his due as a senior and a scholar. Then a man from the French legation was introduced, and the three talked English together as the only language they had in common.

Li watched his chance, and then broadsided the news of his engagement into them. The Frenchman replied with charming enthusiasm, making all the compliments proper to the occasion; the Chinaman gasped, and took the first opportunity to fade away. Li watched him through narrowing eyes.

He saw Mr. Mathers join the group round the cocktail cabinet where Gerald was hard at work shaking, and politely detaching himself from the Frenchman, he drifted across and joined that group, receiving another cocktail from Gerald for his pains, who judged that that was what he had come for. He saw Mr. Mathers look at him with a startled expression, and wondered how much he knew about affairs in the Hope ménage, both domestic and financial. He judged from that startled look that he must know a good deal.

"Hein, Mathers," he said, raising his cocktail glass to him. "Your health."

"Your health, Li," the journalist responded, raising his.

"Thank you, I need it; it is likely to undergo a severe strain in the near future."

"Are you referring to my cocktail-mixing?" laughed Gerald.

"No, your cocktail is excellent. I am referring to the dogs of war, the scorpions, and other domestic animals, with which I expect to be assailed. You have heard of my outrageous conduct, no doubt?"

"I heard something," said Mr. Mathers looking very uncomfortable.

"Don't you think I am a lucky man?"

"I would sooner not express an opinion."

"I don't mind expressing an opinion," said Gerald Conyers, agitating the cocktail shaker with unnecessary vigour. "I think he is damn lucky, and I don't mind who knows it."

Li lifted his glass to the young fellow.

"I drink to you. You are my friend."

"That ought to be good for something," some one said jokingly. "Try him for an overdraft, Gerald. See what his friendship is good for."

"Hein," said Li, "if I say a man is my friend, my friendship is good for all I have got. And if a man says he is my enemy, that is good for all I have got too."

A startled silence fell on the group round the cocktail cabinet, for they saw that Li was speaking in deadly earnest.

Some of them knew of Gerald Conyers' predicament, and had wondered what the presence of the Chinese banker in his house might mean.

"You give me a dare?" cried Li, talking very chi-chi.

"You go into my bank, Conyers, and say to my cashier you want credit, and what is the limit? He will say to you that if Li Wu Lu says you are his friend—or the friend of his wife, there is no limit." He turned to the gasping Mathers. "You go to Mr. Hope and say the same thing—that if a man says he is the enemy of Li Wu Lu—or of his wife, there is no limit either. Thank you, I will have another cocktail." He held out his glass to the dumbfounded Gerald.

He considered it speculatively when it was handed back to him.

"If I had race-horses that won everything, I could marry half a dozen white wives and they would all be received in society. But I do not understand horses. I think they are dangerous wild animals. I know that one end kicks and the other end bites—and that is the extent of my knowledge. No, I do not think I will run race-horses. I think I will put in a swimming-pool at Pei-Chi instead; then when the temperature begins to get up into the eighties, my white wife will be invited to all the parties that are going."

AFTERWORD:

OUT OF THE SHADOWS

by Richard Brzustowicz

THE novels that Violet Mary Firth (1890-1946) published under the name V. M. Steele have long been dismissed by those who write about her as negligible, if not embarrassing. In part, this is because most people who write about her are primarily interested in her career as Dion Fortune, the occultist, and the four novels are not "occult novels". In part, too, it is because the novels deal with issues and situations that are currently often regarded as disreputable or taboo.

Several years ago, I had a chance to stop in London and do some reading in the British Library and the Wellcome Foundation Library. I took the opportunity to look at *The Scarred Wrists* (1935), *Hunters of Humans* (1936), and *Beloved of Ishmael* (1937), the V. M. Steele novels held by the British Library, and the only ones I had ever seen mentioned in connection with Dion Fortune.

Groggy from travel, I still managed to read all three novels. It was immediately clear that they were not, in fact, negligible, and that they should be regarded as a significant component of Violet Firth's writing—as significant as the novels published under the name Dion Fortune. As I read, I took what notes I could, thinking of writing a brief article about them.

After getting back to Seattle, I returned to my notes, intending to write an essay to flesh out the notes before more complete memories of the books faded away. To make sure I had the bibliographic details correct, I checked the entries under V. M. Steele in WorldCat, the library collection database of the Online Computer Library Center (OCLC).

Much to my surprise, I found that there was a fourth V.

M. Steele novel: *The Yellow Shadow*. Few libraries other than the British Library held any of them, and of the few that held the fourth, the National Library of Scotland seemed the most accessible to me.

After some correspondence, and with the gracious assistance of Mr. Gareth Knight, and the permission of the Society of the Inner light (who also were surprised to hear that a fourth V. M. Steele novel existed), and the patient assistance of librarians at the National Library of Scotland, I was able to get a photocopy of The Yellow Shadow. As soon as I read it, I realized that it completely justified my impression of the significance of these novels.

Although The Yellow Shadow was published in 1942, internal evidence suggests that it was written before that, probably before or around 1937. It deals with a China already invaded by Japan (so at least 1932), but before the seizure of Shanghai or the Nanking Massacre (so before 1937) That there is no mention of the Blitz (making it before 1940), nor of the war in Europe (thus before 1938), also suggests a date before 1937. I suspect that the fourth novel was originally intended to follow Beloved of Ishmael (1937); unlike the first three novels, however, the fourth was not (for whatever reason) published by Stanley Paul, and it may be that publication was delayed until 1942 in part due to the need to find another publisher, and in part due to wartime conditions.

Where in China? The presence of discrete foreign communities would suggest Shanghai, but the Battle of Shanghai (1932) and its results do not seem to have influenced the story. Hong Kong would be an obvious alternative, but the island setting is nowhere mentioned, and Hong Kong was very largely British, and did not contain other European concessions. Stella's first Chinese tutor, Mr. Fook, by his name is clearly from the south of China, but whether he taught her Cantonese, or some form of Mandarin, is unclear; if the latter, Stella's ability to understand servants' chatter (unlikely to have been in Mandarin either in Shanghai or Hong Kong) is unexplained.

It is tempting to suppose that the author was simply setting

197

the story "somewhere in China". In other respects, however, she has clearly done her research, and probably relied on consultants who had been in China (perhaps even the very interesting psychiatrist and occultist Dr. Alexander Cannon, with whom she had several acquaintances in common).

Even more intriguing is her acquaintance with the lore about the Bodhisattva Kuan Yin (Guan Yin). Just as the Virgin Mary is associated with the sea (and the name Stella Morris is clearly reminiscent of one of the titles of the Virgin Mary, "Stella Maris", Star of the Sea) so is Kuan Yin. In more recondite lore, Kuan Yin, often manifesting as "fish basket Kuan Yin" is sometimes said to use sexual desire as a "skillful means" to save men who might otherwise be doomed to wander in the world of delusion. It is in this sense, as well as the connection with the sea, that some mythologists have linked Kuan Yin with Aphrodite. In a way quite compatible with the symbolism of Tibetan Buddhism, Stella provides the Wisdom component, and Li the action component, which is finally released and effective in the final scenes of the book.

With this, it is clear that the theme of this novel is not that far from those of *The Sea Priestess, Moon Magic*, or some earlier Dion Fortune novels: the revitalization and enlightenment of an isolated and afflicted man through the wisdom conveyed by a woman who herself embodies supra-personal, divine energies. The difference, perhaps, is that the Dion Fortune novels use romance to sweeten the medicine of explicit occult teaching, while the V. M. Steele novels forego explicit teaching, but nonetheless transmit an initiatory seed through the romance itself.

It is, in other words, the same mind, the same intent, at work through the writings of Violet Mary Firth, Dion Fortune, and V. M. Steele. One cannot properly appreciate Violet Firth's life and work while refusing to engage with the V. M. Steele novels. We are very fortunate that Twin Eagles Publishing has undertaken the task of bringing this book back from exile, to the benefit of everyone.

Made in the USA
Charleston, SC
13 March 2017